The Woman In

CW00447842

I dedicate this book to my amazing frie
I wouldn't be the person I am today withc
me in everything I do and I couldn't be r.

A special thanks also to Alex for helping me along the way.

1

Chapter 1

Abi was just 8 years old when she realised something about her life wasn't quite right. Hearing whispers when no one else did, seeing figures which no one else could see.

Abi had grown up with this being her norm, throughout her teens and into her early twenties, although she never let on to anyone else what she was having to live with.

Growing up she felt so haunted. As soon as she hit 18, she lost the ability to see these spirits and everywhere she went, it felt like someone was watching, but whenever she turned around, no one was to be seen.

7 years later, it is July 10th and the sun is peeping through Abi's blackout blinds, onto her crisp, white cotton bedding where she lay peacefully sleeping. Her fiery locks are a mess of curls surrounding her soft, pale, doll-like face. She had deep hazel eyes that had sparkling gold flecks in the sunlight, but behind those eyes, so many mysteries, so many questions.

Her room was decorated in white and greens with shelves full of books of adventures, history, horror.... you name it, it was there on her shelves.

A collection of crystals displayed beside her bed and plants of all sizes dotted around the room, small succulents on her dresser and window sill, a yuka plant in the corner and a spider plant on one of her many shelves.

Out of the silence, seemingly from across the room, she heard a hushed whisper "Happy birthday... Abigail."
Indeed, it was Abi's 25th birthday today, but where did this voice come from?
She had never heard this voice before. Low and eerie yet somehow it felt scarily familiar. Goosebumps raised all over her body in reaction to this strange voice.
She shook her head and convinced herself that she was still half asleep, rubbed her eyes and rolled out of bed.

She chucked on her favourite black skater dress dotted with glitter, and her labradorite moon pendant that shone like the Aurora Borealis. Sitting at her white dresser, a single succulent plant sat amongst yet more sparkling crystals. She fixed her hair into a high ponytail and applied her make up.

About to stand, she got an all too familiar feeling in the pit of her stomach.
Nervously, she closed her eyes and questioned "Is someone there?" She waited for a couple of seconds and the door behind her started to creak.
She quickly spun around away from her dresser to face the door. Nothing. No-one. Just an empty doorway and part of the hallway.
As she ran her hand over her face, trying to rationalise the door opening, she heard the same voice whisper, as if right next to her at the dressing table, "Help me."

Without looking, she jumped up, grabbed her bag and phone from next to the bed and ran! She flew down the stairs, out of the house, tripping over the loose paving slab at the end of the garden path and ended up on the pavement right in front of Ben.

"Birthday trip?" Ben questioned sarcastically, his black hair moving gently in the summer breeze. His bright blue eyes connected with Abi's terrified, confused expression.
"Very funny, mind helping me up?" She replied.
"Are you okay? You seem shaken."
"Yes, I'm fine, just running late. I'm meant to be meeting my sister and going to my parents for a birthday lunch."

Ben reached out his hand to help Abi up, "Oh yes, you don't want to be late for that, you know your dad likes things running smoothly."
As Ben's strong arms helped her up, Abi winced," Ouch! My ankle. I can't drive like this." She said leaning against the fence, brushing down her dress and noticing her freshly grazed knees.
"Here, I'll drive you," he offered kindly, "It's on my way to work anyway."

They drove down the street to pick up Abi's sister Hannah, Evanescence was singing 'Bring me to life' playing on the radio. The song took her back to her teenage years when she used to hide away down a country lane, she called it her safe space. A place she could go when she was stressed, upset, angry or just needed to breathe. There was a narrow, shallow stream and a small stone bridge that went over it. To the side of the bridge was an old metal fence covered partly by hedgerows, with a small opening that you could just about squeeze through and go sit on the stream bank. It was here she would sit, take out her phone, listen to her music and let the world just pass her by.

Abi grew up with Ben and he always knew when something was up, so he would often accompany Abi down to the stream. He knew how much she struggled, how alone she felt, how she didn't feel like she fitted in. She was different, she just never knew how different.

Ben glanced over at Abi as the song was playing and caught a small smile. He gave her a quizzical look.
"Do you remember the stream?" Abi asked.
Ben's stubbly face softens, "of course! It was so peaceful down there. What was it you called it? your safe space?"
"Yeah." she sighed, "No matter what was going on, I knew that I could go there and no one could judge me or moan at me."

Then out of nowhere, the wing mirror on the passenger side smashed, sending glass fragments through the open window into Abi's face, making them both jump and pulled over abruptly.

"What the hell was that?!" Ben asked out of panic, having slammed on the brakes. "Are you okay?!"
Blood started to trickle down from her right eyebrow, where a piece of glass cut her delicate, pale skin. He rushed out of the car to the boot, to grab the first aid box.

Opening up the box, Ben searched through and found the items he needed.

A quick clean with an alcohol wipe and a small wince on Abi's part, showed only a small cut and nothing to worry too much about.

The only thing they were truly worried about, was what had just happened. HOW did that happen and why?

Chapter 2

They pulled up outside Hannah's house.

A small, cosy cottage with a white picket fence and beautiful red rose bushes on either side of her front door. A typical English countryside home, and it was just that, inside as well as out.
Low ceilings with gorgeous wooden beams and farmhouse décor throughout. It was a country girls dream house.

Hannah came out of the little cottage, helium balloons in the shape of 25 in tow, excited to see her big sister. She was petite in frame, freckles scattered across her small nose onto her rosy cheeks and unlike her sister, she had long brunette hair, but with the same natural waves that every girl dreamed of having. She was only a year younger than Abi and although they had similar features, they couldn't be more different.
Abi was more into the macabre and mysterious, whereas Hannah was the girl into everything pink, baking cupcakes in her fairy-tale style kitchen and having her cake shop in the village called 'Pixies Pastries'.

"Happy birthday!" she screamed, her dainty body running down the garden path. Then realised as she got closer, that it wasn't such a happy birthday so far for poor Abi.

"Oh my god! What happened?" Hannah asked in shock.

Abi looked in the rear-view mirror at herself to see how bad it was. It's not too bad, but they missed a bit of blood when cleaning it as they were already running late to her parents.

"Oh, it's just a scratch, nothing to worry about," she replied, although not completely convincing her sister.

"Hurry up then, jump in the back, we're already late and we're going to make Ben late for work!"

Hannah slid into the back seat, the shiny, purple balloons completely hiding the fact she was there.

"Sorry to make you late Ben, how is it that we're riding with you anyway? Is your car playing up again Abi?"

Ben replied, "Don't worry, I'm not late yet. Your sister decided to fall at my feet this morning!"

"Oh you think you're so funny, don't you! I didn't fall at his feet, I tripped over that paving slab I keep meaning to fix and I hurt my ankle. Mr funny here offered to take us on his way to work as I couldn't drive myself."

"Oh Abi," Hannah sighed, "Are you sure that house is safe? It's so old and you have so much to do to it."

Abi lived in a Victorian house located on Old England road, where most houses were from the Victorian era. This particular house was in a Gothic Revival style from the 1800s, with a tower at the front, a porch that stretched across the front of the house and beautiful, big bay windows.

Abi loved the Gothic style architecture and couldn't let this opportunity to own such an incredible, breathtaking home pass her by. Okay, it needed a lot of work, but Abi didn't mind.

She did most of the renovations herself and brought back its 1850's glory with dark coloured rooms, cosy lighting and grand fireplaces, (apart from her light and airy bedroom that is).

Even though she was alone in this house, she never quite felt that was the case. She would often catch a glimpse of a shadow in the reflection of the gold-framed mirror above the fireplace, whilst sealing the brickwork on the chimney breast, or an outline of a person standing behind her in the shine from the green tiles in the bathroom.

But like her sister said, she still had a lot to do. The kitchen cabinets need fitting, the garden re-landscaping and the tower library hadn't even been started.

"I know it's old, that's why I love it. I'm almost done with the renovations now. I have a carpenter in next week to fit the kitchen cabinets and I'm starting the library tomorrow which hopefully won't take too long. I just need to build the shelves, lay the carpet, add some cushions to the bay window seat and unpack my books, then all that's left is the garden." Abi explained, standing by her decision to buy this spectacular house.

"I have 2 weeks off from work as of tomorrow, if you need a hand." Ben offered, and secretly he wanted the excuse to be around Abi more anyway.
"Really?! That would be amazing, thank you so much!" Abi squealed in excitement, as they pulled up outside her parent's house.
"Is 9 am too early? I'll have a fried breakfast waiting for you!" she bargained.
"Oh go on then, you've twisted my arm, you know I can't resist an English brekkie!" Ben said whilst laughing.
"Haha thank you! You're the best! I'll see you in the morning then." Abi replied happily, as she climbed out of the car and brushed any remaining glass from her seat. "Sorry again about the mirror, no idea what happened but thank you for playing Doctor," she said playfully. She closed the door and gave a little wave as she walked up to her parent's home, she just hoped nothing else would go wrong today.

Chapter 3

Her parents lived in a quiet cul-de-sac in the countryside. A small bungalow with a beautiful garden filled with flowers, a little vegetable patch and her mum's sewing room that looked out over rolling fields. On occasion, she would get a couple of visits from the horses passing by, hoping for a crunchy carrot.

Abi's parents were already at the door waiting for her as she and her sister made their way down the path.

Her mum was smaller in height and curvy, but had the same warm red hair as Abi, only shorter and curlier. She wore her hair half up half down and the ends just about touched her shoulders. A pen stuck in her ponytail and a set of silver reading glasses sat on top of her head.

Abi's dad was a giant of a man. Standing 6 foot 2, black hair with pepper greys scattered throughout and showing the early stages of ageing.

"Happy birthday darling." her mum, Jenny said with a warm embracing hug.
"And what time do you call this?' Her dad Greg asked, trying to be funny.
"Hi Dad," Abi replied with a smile.
"Sorry we're running late, I had a fall outside the house and Ben had to give us a lift as I hurt my ankle," Abi explained.

Jenny and Greg both noticed the cuts on her face and knees, assuming it to be just from where she fell.

Abi was just grateful that she didn't have to try and explain that one to them.

Her dad didn't believe in anything paranormal, unlike the 3 women of the family. Abi, her mum and her sister used to love sitting on the sofa in the evening and watching 'Most Haunted' together. But every time one of the psychics got involved, he would just laugh and try to explain how it's all fake and mediums lie to get your money etc.

It wound Abi up a lot.

She had had her own experiences growing up, which her mum knew of and knew Abi was gifted, but Greg wouldn't have any of it.

As a result, Abi grew up not being able to talk about her experiences. Like when she saw a glowing shadow at the end of her bed, and the next day her dog died, or going to the well-known Screaming Woods at night with her friends, and seeing a figure hanging from a tree, that of course, wasn't there. The next day her friend's friend committed suicide.

These were no coincidences in her life.

Abi's childhood and teenage years were full of these memories, but she hadn't seen anything like this since she was 18 and it was such a relief.

The four of them went inside and were greeted by the most excited, slobbery St. Bernard, Zeus. Abi had named him as a puppy and she loved Greek mythology, so she just had to pick a Greek god name!

After her slobber attack, Abi made her way to the kitchen to clean off. Out of the window, she saw all of her family in the garden with balloons, food, cake, the lot! "Surprise!" They all shouted excitedly.

"Oh no!" Abi thought, as she felt her cheeks going bright red. Abi hated being the centre of attention and would always get so embarrassed.

She made her way around the balloon infested garden, she made small talk with Uncle Todd, who was a bit of a strange one, to be honest. He would always repeat the same stories about celebrities he had met on his holiday to the famous L.A. To be honest, it's pretty much the only thing that had any excitement in his life.

He lived alone with a cat called Timothy, and very rarely left his home, apart from his one trip that he had won through a radio advertisement.

9

Trying to avoid another reminder of the time he met Johnny Depp, Abi gave her sister a quick 'SAVE ME' look across the garden.

Hannah knew how much Abi hated social gatherings, and how she always felt awkward having to make small talk with people, even family.

Hannah shouted across the lawn, "Hey Abi, give me a hand will you?!"
Abi apologised to Uncle Todd and made her way over to her sister, a look of relief crossed her face and mouthed the words 'Thank God' as she walked away.

"Here, this should help," Hannah said, passing Abi a bottle of strawberry and lime cider.
"Perfect! Thank you. I wish mum wouldn't organise surprise parties. I was looking forward to a nice BBQ with just the 4 of us. Maybe a little sunbathing and a water fight?" She slumped down into a plastic garden chair to the side of the garden, hoping she would go unnoticed.

She gazed around at the 15 odd members of the family dotted around the lawn, when she noticed someone in the kitchen window. She looked familiar but couldn't pinpoint exactly who she was.

"Who's that in the kitchen?" She turned to ask Hannah whilst having another sip of her cider.
Hannah looked over to the kitchen window and didn't see anyone there.
"What are you talking about? There's no one there? Are you sure you didn't sneak a few drinks this morning and that's why you were running late and fell over?" Hannah giggled.
Abi turned back around to look, and Hannah was right, there was no one to be seen.

Abi stood to go check it out, but as soon as she was upright, the world started to spin and she passed out in a heap on the grass.

As she laid on the grass, family surrounded her in panic.
She dreamed.

A lady... who looked amazingly like her.
She wore a silk dress, which seemed very impractical with its wide skirt and tight-fitting bodice, pulled so tight that she could barely breathe.

The Woman In The Mirror

She was walking along a river. The land seemed very familiar. Like she had been there before. There was a figure walking towards her, but she couldn't make out who it was. A black shadow person came closer and closer until she heard a banshee-like scream and woke suddenly, dripping with sweat.

As she sat straight up, terrified from her dream, she realised she was in her old room, which had been turned into the guest room.
Surrounding her were boxes of childhood toys and memorabilia, including boxes filled with photo albums and frames.
But the one thing that stood out to Abi, was the photo on the wall opposite. Faded sepia but certainly the woman from her dream!

Jenny came rushing into the room after hearing a scream. The scream wasn't just in Abi's dream; it was Abi screaming.
"Abi! What's wrong?! Are you okay?" Jenny asked frantically, worried about her daughter.
"Who is that in the photo?" Abi asked, completely bypassing Jenny's concern.
Puzzled, Jenny replied "That is your great grandmother from the 1800s, Katrina Taylor. Stories say she just disappeared one day, leaving her husband to care for their new-born baby."

Jenny grabbed one of the many boxes surrounding them and popped it on the bed next to them.
Rummaging around, she found what she was looking for and pulled out a single photograph of a tall man in a suit, holding a cane. His eyes seemed dark and he had a moustache that curled at both ends.
"This is James Taylor, her husband. Did you know our family was of quite importance back then? James had painted for Queen Victoria and even painted a portrait of her which is now kept in a museum in London. We took you there once when you were about 8 years old. You loved seeing all the paintings and you've been so creative ever since. I like to think maybe your talent and creativity was passed down from James."

Abi was an interior designer by day and artist in her spare time. For as long as she could remember, she had always loved painting and designing, with some of her work even being admired in local magazines.

Out of all of her memories, she could not remember this outing with her family, but she was so young at the time.

Abi couldn't shake the feeling that her dream and these photos were all connected, but why would she be having them? She shrugged it off.
As interesting as it all was, it just didn't make sense. As she had only dreamt this once, it's just a coincidence, right?

"You look pale, I'll go and get you a glass of water. We've sent everyone home so don't worry about people still being here, just relax sweetheart."
Jenny left the bedroom, shutting the door behind her to ensure the room was nice and quiet for Abi.

While her mum was getting her a drink, Abi pulled the box of photos closer to have a nose through them. The box was completely mixed up with current photos, childhood photos and photos like those of her ancestors.
She started arranging the photos on the bed and ended up with 3 piles to look through, but of course, she was only really interested in one pile.

She started looking through the handful of old, sepia photos. Faded over time and some with rips at the corners from being handled over the years.
The first seemed to be of Katrina and James on their wedding day.
Katrina wore a white dress made with a mix of lace, silk and tulle with a corset pulled tight enough to show her tiny waist and a cathedral length veil made from fine lace. Upon her head sat the most beautiful diamond and pearl tiara, given to her by her husband. She wore a dainty pair of white gloves and held a big bouquet of blossoms.

James was dressed in a white waistcoat, a morning coat tailored especially with a special flower hole and flower to match Katrina's bouquet and finished with his very best top hat.

For a couple who had just got married, you'd think they would look happier. Katrina seemed to force a smile, but her eyes looked sad and James didn't even have a smile at all. He had such a vague expression on his face, as if he didn't care whether he was married or not.
This was meant to be the happiest day of their lives and instead, it looked as though someone had died.

The 2nd photo Abi picked up was of Katrina, James and their baby boy Henry. Again, this family of 3 didn't seem happy. Were people not allowed to smile in photos or were they just this unhappy? Abi wondered.

Jenny returned to the room with a glass of water for Abi, ice clinking against the glass as she closed the door behind her.
"Find anything interesting?" she asked.
"I don't understand why in every photo they look so unhappy" Abi replied with a hint of confusion in her voice and a puzzled look across her brow.

She passed the old family photos over to Jenny to see for herself.

"Oh, I hadn't come across these yet. They certainly were a beautiful family, weren't they? But yes, I see what you mean. Thing is, times were different back then. A lot of women married for a better life rather than love. You had to marry in the same class as yourself or higher. If you married a lower class, then you were looked at as though you married beneath you. It just wasn't the done-thing. But who knows..."
Jenny popped the photos back into the box.
"If you like, you can take these home with you if you're interested in them." Jenny offers.
"'Yeah, sure," Abi replied, trying to not sound too interested, but of course she was. They were the link to the dream she just had, what if there was more to find out?

Abi reached for her glass, but misjudging the distance, knocked the water all over the box of photos. They quickly emptied the box as fast as they could and got the photos in the sunlight to dry.

"I am so sorry Mum, I don't know what's going on with me today," Abi said apologetically.
"Is the house stressing you out darling? Have you taken on too much?" Jenny replied with concern.
"No, of course not. The house is coming along really well and I'm almost done. Even Ben has offered to help me over the next few weeks as he has time off from work." Abi explained.
"Okay. Well, I'm glad Ben is helping you out. He's such a kind lad. You've done so much of the house on your own, you need a rest. You'll make yourself ill if you're not careful."
"I know, I'll be careful," Abi replied to get her mum off her back.

"Now, what do you want to do about dinner? You can stay here if you like or I can get your dad to take you home so you can rest up?" Jenny said as she made her way back to the bedroom door.

"Could Dad take me home, please? I need to make sure I'm rested and ready for when Ben comes to help me in the morning. I offered to make him breakfast if he came round early."

"Of course, wouldn't want to let the handsome man down would we Abi, you're not getting any younger dear," Jenny said with a wink, just as Abi threw a cushion her way.

Chapter 4

Greg pulled up outside Abi's home.

Abi kissed her dad on the cheek, "Thank you for bringing me home. I'm sorry today didn't go as planned. I think mum's right; I need to get some rest."
"We do worry about you kiddo," he said, pulling her in for a hug. "I know you've not had a great birthday but please try and get some rest okay."
"I will" Abi replied as she pulled away from the hug to get out of the car.
"Bye Dad, Love you."
"Love you too," Greg replied, re-adjusting his seat belt.

As she walked down the hazardous path, remembering to step over the lethal paving slab, she spotted a long white box to the side of the door waiting for her on the porch. She picked it up and read the note that was stuck to the front.

Happy birthday Abi, the Doctor will see you in the morning!

"Ben, you idiot." She thought, feeling her body fill with warmth and a big grin appear on her face.
She popped her bag down beside her and opened the box to find the most beautiful bouquet of sunburst orange roses.
She brought the box close to her chest in appreciation and a became overwhelmed..

The Woman In The Mirror

She opened the door and walked into the dark hallway, locking the door and placing her keys in the glass bowl that resided on the small table beside the door.
The silence was deafening.
"I think it's time I get a pet for company," she whispered to herself.

She walked through to the kitchen and put the lovely bouquet of orange roses and white baby's breath into a glass vase on the windowsill.

She then grabbed the bottle of White Zinfandel wine from the fridge and a mug from one of the many boxes she'd yet to unpack. She poured herself a large measure and took it to the back garden, where the sky was just starting to fill with warm orange and soft reds as the sun began to set on her birthday.

As she sat on the bench, looking over her garden, she couldn't help but think about all the things she needed to do with it. She shook her head, "Mums right, I need to rest!"
She finished her mug of wine in a big gulp and headed back into the kitchen. She popped her mug in to the empty sink, to wash the next day.

She made her way down the hall and started heading up the creaky stairs to go to bed.

'I just need an early night.' she said to herself, hand sliding along the wooden bannister.
She walked along the dark landing and into her oasis bedroom.
This was the one room in the house that didn't keep in with the Victorian decor.
She wanted this space to be a light, airy, relaxing space with a clean energy.

She closed the blinds and pulled the curtains, flooding the room with darkness.
She popped her lamp on, got changed into her silky cami set and climbed into bed.
As soon as her head hit the pillow, she was out like a light.

And she dreamed...

It was 1857. A lady dressed in the deepest green silk dress, corset pulling in at her waist and a skirt as puffy as candy floss. Red curly hair pinned up and beautiful deep green eyes that sparkled in the sun.

The Woman In The Mirror

She was sat on a bench in a large country park, reading a book about a lady who conceived a daughter through an affair, who now had to wear the letter "A" for adultery, on her clothes and is shamed publicly as she struggles to create a new life. She is distracted by the children running and playing around her on the green. How she longed to have a child of her own.

She was 22, a year above the marrying age.

Her parents urged her to find a worthy husband, but failing to do so, her father would set up a meeting with one of his business associates to introduce their son.

A tall handsome gentleman she had not met before approaches.

'May I?' he gestured to the space next to her on the bench.
'Certainly', she replied.
They engaged in conversation about literature and the arts.
He revealed himself as an artist for the Queen and she is completely taken aback.
'I could paint your portrait if you like?' he offered.
'Oh I am nothing special,' she replied.
'But of course you are, you are beautiful.'
She felt her cheeks start to blush.

The dream started to fade into another...

Blue and green colours slowly swirled with flickers of sunlight shining through.
Peaceful, tranquil.
But then suddenly, the water started rushing and bubbling around her. Fighting for her breath, she screamed through the depths.

Abi awoke, still screaming.
Her heart was racing and for a moment, still thought she was dreaming as she heard the gushing of water.
She rubbed her face and realised she was in fact, awake.

She dragged her feet onto the cold, hard, dark wood floor.
She tapped the switch for her lamp, but it didn't turn on.
"Great, no power. Because this isn't creepy at all is it!" she said out loud to herself.
She picked up her phone and switched the torchlight on, almost blinding herself in the process.

Taking a deep breath, she started to approach her bedroom door.

She slowly turned the doorknob and opened the heavy door out onto the dark, still landing.

She walked out gently onto the landing, her hands gliding across the walls and headed in the direction of the running water.

The bathroom.

As she approached the bathroom, she saw the light on through the window above the door and water coming from underneath.

She turned the old, brass doorknob and pushed the door open.

Water overflowed the deep, black, brass footed bathtub.

Abi rushed in to turn off the taps but no matter how much she twisted and turned them, the water wouldn't stop running.

She knew she would have to turn off the water completely but as she took her next step, she slipped on the wet tiled surface and hit her head as she landed, leaving her unconscious in a puddle of water.

The water stopped running!

Chapter 5

It was 8.50 am and Ben was 10 minutes early. He grabbed the brass knocker and tapped it against the door.
No answer.
He went around the back to see if she was in the garden, but there was no sign of Abi.
He turned the handle to the back door and it opened. He must remind her to keep her doors locked.
"Abi?!" He called out. Still no reply.

He checked the downstairs rooms for her, but she was nowhere in sight.

Drip... Drip.

"Water?" He questioned, as he noticed a puddle forming in the middle of the floor.
He headed up the old, grand staircase and onto the landing, when he saw the water on the floor leading to the bathroom.
He headed to the bathroom, water squelching beneath his feet and reached out to open the door, but something was behind it.
He managed to squeeze his head through the gap to see what was stopping him from pushing the door open.
"ABI!!" He cried out.

19

Squeezing through the gap and kneeling to the water-logged floor, he checked her heart rate.

She's alive!

Gently tapping on her collar bones and calling her name, she woke up.

Her clothes were soaked through, her hair dripping from the water she had been laying in, making her curls straight from the heaviness of the water absorbed in it and a pounding headache from where she hit her head.

"Abi are you okay?! What happened? Do we need to take you to the hospital?" Ben asked, with panic in his voice.
"I don't know," she replied. "I heard water in the night and when I saw it coming from here, I tried to turn the taps off, but the water just kept coming. I must have slipped."
She tried to sit up and the bathroom started to spin.
"Oh my head!" she put her head in both hands, in hopes it would stop the motion.
"Here," Ben said, putting his arm around her and picking her up in both arms.

He carried her out of the flooded bathroom, along the water-drenched hall and back to bed placing a cold, damp flannel on her head.
"I'm just going to get you some painkillers and a glass of water, although I'm sure you've had enough water for one day." he tried to joke to make light of the situation.

Abi laid in her bed, her head against her soft, duck feather pillows. "What the hell was happening?" She thought.
Her whole body felt heavy and exhausted, she could feel her eyelids starting to close and she was back in another dream.

The same lady from before, but this time she wore a navy blue, silk dress with white lace embellishments. A blue-ribbon choker around her neck. Pearl drop earrings hung from her perfectly small ears and her hair was set in ringlets, in a half up half down style.

She was sitting in a wood-panelled room, a chandelier hanging above, seemed to be decorated with diamonds that flickered light around the room.
She sat on a chair with a book in her hands.

She was having her portrait painted.

And by the handsome stranger she had met in the park. But he was no longer a stranger. She felt like she had known him her whole life.
She laughed at his jokes while he set up his easel.

He started mixing paints on the canvas to create a soft, peaceful background to make her stand out and her beauty shine through.
He started with a pale blue, then mixed in some titanium white and blending ripples of pale green.

Abi sensed a pattern, a repetition of what happened in her last dream and woke abruptly, just as Ben was bringing in food, water and painkillers.

On a tray, he had brought in a cooked breakfast, like she was meant to be cooking for him this morning, a glass of water and some paracetamol for her head.
"Oh you didn't have to do this Ben, I was meant to be doing breakfast for you this morning, not the other way around!" she said guiltily.
"Don't be silly, you're not doing anything today. You need to rest. I can still get on with what I'm meant to be doing here whilst you sleep. Just tell me what needs to be done." He replied, more than happy to look after her and help out.
"If you could make a start on the tower library that would be great! All the shelves are laid out on the floor. I've already marked out where they need to be fitted, so they just need putting up and the carpet needs to be laid."

"Okay, sounds easy enough. I've brought my tools with me so I don't need to find yours. Anything else you need looking at today?" He asked.
"Oh if you could look at the bathroom taps that would be great! Thank you for switching the water off this morning. You saved me and the house from flooding." She replied gratefully.
"Abi, I didn't shut off the water. There wasn't any water running when I got here. The bath was empty and you were just laying in a puddle on the floor." Ben said, a little confused and started to worry she might have a concussion.
"Are you sure we don't need to take you to the hospital?" Ben questioned again.
"No," Abi replied, frowning and confused. "No, I think I just need to sleep."
"Only if you are sure Abi, it's not a problem, I don't mind taking you."
"No, no. I'll be okay. Go, get on with the library before I fire you." she joked with the smallest of smiles that she could muster up.

"Yes Ma'am," He laughed and headed out the door.

Chapter 6

Ben walked along the landing to the tower door.
The door was a thick, dark oak wood with an ornate brass doorknob and an old brass key in the lock.
He turned the key and the lock clicked.
He twisted the handle and opened the door to reveal a spiral staircase.
The staircase was bare and dusty, with a single arched window to let in light.
As he got to the top of the tower, there was another doorway that opened up into the library room.

It was a fairly big room, with wooden panel walls and paintings that he assumed Abi had painted. The ceiling was decorated in mesmerising Artex and a brass chandelier in the middle.

Over in the corner, the carpet roll was leaning against the wall waiting to be laid and the bookshelves placed out, ready to be made up.
The shelving units were the same dark coloured wood as the walls, so once up, they would look as though they are built-in.

Some of the furnishings were also up there set to one side, including a chaise longue in royal blue velvet, a carved oak coffee table and a round, gold-framed mirror which had to be around a metre and a half in size.

Ben got to work starting with the bookcase.

It didn't take him long and as soon as he knew where each piece was meant to be, he was whizzing through.

Ben enjoyed a bit of DIY. He knew so many people who would get agitated and lose their patience when doing DIY, but he found it therapeutic.

Turning around to pick up the next shelf to fit in the bookcase, he caught a glimpse of Abi in the mirror that sat on the chaise longue.

"Abi, what are you doing out of bed? I told you to get some sleep."

He turned around to look at her after picking up the shelf, but she was not there.

She must have just been checking in quickly and gone back to bed, he thought. He decided to pop downstairs to check that she was okay and see if she needed anything.

He opened her bedroom door quietly and there she lay, asleep.

"Strange." he thought.

A slither of light peeked through her curtains and onto her soft, pale skin. Ben stood there fro a moment, thinking how beautiful she was and how he admired her. She worked for herself. She was talented, smart... and so beautiful.

He closed the door gently behind him and put the events that happened in the library, down to his brain playing tricks on him.

He went back to the library, popped some music on and put his earphones in.
Bon Jovi sang 'It's my life' and Ben playing air guitar with one of the final shelves.
He finished his guitar solo and slotted the shelf into place. He stepped back to admire the bookcase, when he heard his name being spoken in his earphones.

"Bennn." A voice said in a hushed whisper, as Bon Jovi finished singing.

As fast as he could, he ripped the earphones from his ears, chucked them on the floor and just stared at them. He then felt a cold breeze on his neck and quickly spun around.

It was mid-summer, there was no wind, besides, none of the windows were open either.

His heart started to race, but his body was frozen to the spot.

Downstairs, Abi had woken up from a deep silent sleep. She felt so much better. Headache gone and feeling more alive, she got dressed. Dungaree shorts and an old t-shirt with sunflowers on it.

She scraped her hair back into a messy bun, popped on some lipstick and mascara and headed up to the library to see how Ben was getting on.

She got to the top of the stairs and saw Ben standing there, not moving a muscle.
"Ben... what's wrong? You look like you've seen a ghost." She questioned.
"This is going to sound stupid, but you have to believe me," he said, trying not to sound like a maniac.
"Earlier, I thought I saw you in the mirror, but when I turned around you weren't there, so I went downstairs to check on you and you were fast asleep. I came back up, finished the bookshelf and that was when I heard someone whisper my name... in my earphones!" he explained to her, completely knowing how this sounded and hoping Abi wouldn't think he was mental.

"I believe you," she replied.
"You do?" He said in relief.
"Yes. Yesterday morning just as I was waking up, I heard someone whisper happy birthday to me and they used my full name and no one calls me by my full name. Then before I bumped into you yesterday, I heard the same voice whisper "help me" and it sounded like it came from my mirror."
"Bumped into me? You mean fell at my feet right?" Ben said, trying to sound more like himself.
"Ben, I'm serious. That's the reason I came running out of my house in the first place. And then for your wing mirror to smash in my face. Then at mums yesterday, I saw a woman in the kitchen, but when I asked my sister who it was, the woman had disappeared and I passed out when I started to investigate. Something really weird is going on. And I'm having the strangest dreams as well."
"What dreams?" Ben asked, hoping to try and make some sense out of all this madness.
"There's a woman who looks like me, but she's in Victorian dress. But she looks like the woman in the photos my mum showed me."
"Really?! Do you have the photos?" He asked in disbelief.
"No, they're at my mums. I was going to bring the box back with me but I spilled my water all over them, so we had to lay them out to dry. I can see if they can drop the photos round though." She said as she took out her phone.

Abi dialled her mum's phone number into her phone and pressed call.

"Hi Mum."
"Hi hunnie, how are you feeling today?" Jenny asked.

"A lot better thanks, had a lot of help from Ben and he even demanded I stay in bed to get some rest while he put together the bookcase for me." Abi knew she was lying to her mum but if she knew the truth she would never hear the end of it.

"Oh what a lovely lad. You know you could do worse, Abi. He seems hubby material to me."

THANK GOD she didn't put her mum on loudspeaker!

"Mum, how did the photos turn out? Did they dry okay? I was hoping maybe you could pop them over so I could show Ben once we finish the library."

"Yes that's fine, I need to go shopping so I'll drop them off on the way," Jenny replied.

"Great, thanks Mum. I'll see you soon."

"Bye sweetheart."

"Great, Mum's going to drop the box of photos off on her way to the shops."

"Cool. While we wait for your mum then, shall we get this carpet fitted?" Ben asked, trying to get some normality back.

"Yeah sure," Abi said, walking over to the carpet laying up against the wall. The carpet was a fluffy, deep blue to match the chaise longue.

She started to drag the carpet away from the wall, but lost her footing and ended up falling into Ben, sending them both to the floor and landing on top of him.

She lifted up slightly, one hand on her forehead, "I'm so sorry, are you okay? I'm so clumsy!"

"That's okay," he replied, not minding the physical contact at all.

"I seem to have that effect on you don't I? You're either falling at my feet or falling on me," he said with a cheeky smile.

"No I'm not," she said, feeling her cheeks starting to redden. She quickly gets up and dusts herself off. She couldn't tell whether she was embarrassed or giddy but she definitely had butterflies around him.

Ben leant down and rolled the carpet out. Only a few of the edges needed cutting which was lucky!

As they were finishing the last part of the carpet, they heard Jenny call up the stairs, "Are you both decent?!"

"Mum! Oh my god, we're laying the carpet nothing else!" she said, and this time she was most definitely embarrassed!

"Well I don't know, do I? You're both young. Both attractive. It's not that unthinkable really. Anyway, I have the box of photos you wanted. Where would you like them?" Jenny asked.

"Just pop them down in the bay window seat for now and I'll sort them out later. Thank you for bringing them over." Abi said.

"Not a problem at all. Well, I've got some shopping to do. I'll let myself out and leave you two to... well... whatever it was you were up to." Jenny said playfully.

"Laying the carpet mum."

"Yep, if that's what you youngsters call it these days. Bye Abi, Bye Ben. Look after my baby." Jenny replied with a wave, as she walked down the tower stairs to let herself out.

"Oh my god! I am so sorry! That was so embarrassing. Please just ignore her?!" Abi begged Ben. At this point, she just wanted the ground to just swallow her whole.

"That's okay. My mum's just the same. I think it's just something they feel they have to do as we get older."

Ben passed the Stanley knife, used to cut the carpet, to Abi, " All done."

Abi reached out to take the knife from him, to chuck back in the toolbox next to her. Their fingers touched and they both felt a tingle go down their spines. As they looked at each other the box of photos fell to the floor with a loud bang and a single photo slid out onto the carpet.

Katrina.

Chapter 7

Ben picked up the photo, he reached for it slowly and picked it up like it had a disease.

He held the photo up and compared it against Abi. It was so much like her that it could actually be the same person. As if Abi had gone to a fancy dress party dressed in Victorian attire.

"This is incredible," Ben said, amazed by the photo he held in his hands. He couldn't stop looking back and forth from the photo to Abi like he was watching a tennis match.

Left. Right. Left. Right.

"But what does it mean?" Ben asked.

"I'm not sure yet. I'm hoping maybe you could help me work out what's going on. I want to find out more about Katrina. I think maybe she is behind everything. The whispers, the mirror smashing, the water in the bathroom and these dreams, it's the only thing that makes sense." Abi replied.

"Of course I'll help, but what can I do?" Ben said, feeling excited but also a bit scared at the same time. Did he want to know the answer to this question? Not really. But there was no way on earth he was going to let Abi go through this on her own.

"I was wondering... I don't have any internet yet so I was thinking, maybe we could go to yours and do some research and see what we come up with. Where had she lived, how old was she etc? Maybe even look into seeing how we could monitor any activity here and get some answers." Abi suggested. Also, it gets them out of this house. She was starting to feel unsafe after what happened last night, so being in a different environment would make her feel a lot more at ease.

"Yeah, that's not a problem at all. Great idea." He said, trying to cover up the fact that the idea of monitoring activity and searching for ghosts, really gave him the creeps. All the hairs on his arms and the back of his neck stood on end.
Were they really going to do this?
Were they actually looking for ghosts now?

Ben put all of his tools away and picked up his heavy metal toolbox and grabbed his keys.

Abi picked up her laptop, the box of photos, a note pad and some pens and chucked them in a bag. She balanced them all one on top of the other. Laptop on the bottom, then the box, then the bag with the notepad and pens and carries them to the front door. With one hand on the door handle and the other balancing all of her items, she took one last glance around and headed out of the door.

As soon as she stepped outside, she felt a wave of relief roll over her, as she was no longer in the house worrying about what was going to happen next. And if anything did happen, then at least she wasn't alone.

Ben only lived a couple of doors down, another bonus, and his house was just as beautiful as Abi's, only he didn't have the renovations to do. His home was decorated with a very modern taste, not a lot of colour, mainly whites, pale greens and pine wood.

Abi hadn't been in Ben's house. Although they had been friends since they were children, they hadn't been around each other for about 5 months and it was at that time that Ben had bought his house and Abi about 2 months later. With work and the renovations, Abi hadn't had a chance to visit him. They would talk via text and see each other in passing and stop for a quick chat, but as much as they wanted to talk for longer, she was just so busy.

She walked in his front door and was quite surprised by how clean and smart his home was. She was imagining a proper bachelor pad with a stag head above the fireplace, a brown leather sofa, sports trophies on the shelves and a big cinema size TV screen, But it wasn't like that at all.

Actually, it reminded her more of a showroom.

Pine wooden flooring, black leather sofa with white fluffy cushions and a knitted throw, a white fluffy footstool, 40 inch TV above the fireplace and white candles on the mantle. A spider plant in a basket sat in the corner of the room and 3 succulent plants on the glass coffee table in the middle of the room on a silver tray. The table sat on top of a large, you guessed it, white fluffy rug.

Abi put her stuff down, took her shoes off and walked through to the living room with her laptop under her arm.

"Nice house you've got," she comments, admiring the white marble fireplace. "Thanks. The house actually came like this so I've not had to do anything. Even has underfloor heating for in the winter when it's cold." Ben replied, trying to impress.

Abi was impressed with the underfloor heating, as she despised feeling cold in any way, but she felt the home could have a personal touch. As nice as it was, it just looked like it was straight out of a home interiors magazine.

"Why don't I fix us up some lunch while you get that laptop fired up? The WiFi password is on top of the mantel," Ben said. "Bacon and Brie Panini?"
"Sounds great!" Abi replied, her mouth-watering at the thought. It was one of Abi's favourites, although she hadn't had one in a long time.

Abi sat herself down on the sofa, making sure to put the blanket underneath her. She hated leather. You stick to it in the summer and it's freezing cold to touch in the winter. The sofa would be the first thing she would change if she was to ever redesign his living space.

Sat with her laptop, she typed into the Google search bar, Katrina Taylor, and hit the search button.
Up popped at least 1000 different Katrina's. There must be an easier way to find her. Instead she searched, James Taylor artist.
The Google results all showed the right person and listings of his paintings, the museum that homes his paintings and news articles.

She decided to click on news articles.
There were many!

The first painter under 20 to paint for Queen Victoria.
Young artist wins award for life-like painting.

Young upcoming artist of the year.
Artist James Taylor marries beautiful Katrina.
Artist James Taylor becomes a father!
James Taylor left to care for baby as his wife disappears.

JACKPOT!

Abi clicked on the final link, James Taylor left to care for baby as his wife disappears. The article loaded with a black and white photo of James holding his son, standing next to a painting of the once family of three.

2 May 1860

James Taylor left to care for the baby as his wife disappears.

On Tuesday 1st May, Katrina Taylor was reported missing from their home on England Street, for 24 hours.
James Taylor states he was at a customers house at the time of the disappearance, working on a painting.
He returned home to find Baby Henry with the nanny and no sign of Katrina.
The nanny, Miss Helen Watson, confirms that Katrina had gone for a walk in the park around 11 am and never came home.
James confesses that Katrina had many issues that they were trying to deal with.
Police are questioning neighbours and have asked if anyone has any information, then to please get in contact as soon as possible.
They believe she may be of danger to herself.

Just below the last sentence was a black and white portrait of Katrina.

"Whoa!" Abi said a bit too loudly, making Ben jump while he's cooking the bacon.
"What is it?" He asked, pretending to be un-phased by her sudden reaction out of nowhere.
"They think Katrina had mental issues when she disappeared. They said they believed she may be of danger to herself."
"Hmm, seems a bit odd though don't you think. Back then, if you were believed to have issues then weren't you put in like, an insane asylum?" Ben questioned.
"Yeah, you'd think that wouldn't you. And I believe there was one just outside of London. Let me check quick." She quickly typed Victorian asylum London into the search bar.

It came up straight away.

Blue waters - County Asylums

Built in 1830 and took on 24 male patients and 18 female, but the population grew over the decades.
Blue waters was built in a neo-classical style with octagonal towers and arched windows and doors.
Blue Waters had a reputation of having more people leave in boxes rather than walking out the front door alive.
The most used method of treatment at the asylum was 'Cold water treatment'.

This was used in 2 ways.

Cold baths and also being chained to the spot and having cold water thrown over you.
One doctor even claimed that this was the most successful method for treating violently insane and bad behaviour.

"I don't think I can read any more of this! It's inhumane what they did to those poor people!" Abi complained, feeling both sorrow and anger for the way people were treated back then.

Ben passed her a plate with a fresh, hot bacon and brie panini.

She took it from him, not overly sure whether she still felt hungry after reading the article on the asylum. She still thanked him though and it did smell delicious.

"So, do you know if she had been in the asylum yet?" Ben asked.
"No, not yet. I've just read a little about the history and the methods used, which I wish I hadn't." She continued, "I can't seem to find much on Katrina. There are lots of articles about James and his artwork career, but not much about her." Abi said in frustration.

Abi picked up her panini, cheese oozing from the side. "mmmmm," Abi sounded, the taste of the saltiness from the bacon and the creaminess from the cheese filling her mouth. "This is delicious!"

"You... are... welcome!" Ben replied.

Ben picked up the photo of Katrina with one hand whilst eating his panini with the other.
"There has to be another way we can find out more about her. " He thought.
Then he remembered a video his friend posted on Youtube.
His friend Jack was a paranormal investigator with his own Youtube channel.

He grabbed the laptop from Abi and quickly brought up Youtube and typed his friend's name into the search bar.

He clicked on the latest video and pressed play.

It begins with Jack saying hi to everyone and telling them where they are and explaining that lots of activity is happening in the house, so he's there to find out who and why they are haunting this young family.

Further along in the video, they try an experiment.
A lady sits in front of a mirror.
They were sitting in complete darkness.

Another woman in the background had a brass singing bowl in her hand. She hits the side of it with a small mallet then circles the edges and it makes a calming sound as it sends vibrations and energy into the air.

The woman in the chair stares into her reflection for about 2 minutes and her head suddenly drops forward!
The medium who was holding the singing bowl is now by the ladies side and asking her questions.

"Who are you?" The medium asks.
The lady's head slowly repositions to looking straight ahead and her eyes open wide.
"Sarah." She replies in an unusual voice, not of her own.
"Why are you here?" The medium asks.
"Home." The spirit replies.

"This is not your home anymore, This is Adam and Lucy's home now." The medium responds.

"Where is my sister?" the spirit asks.

"Who is your sister?"

After a few minutes of absolute silence, she finally replies

"Andrea." and then the lady's head drops back down and she comes to.

"Lucy, are you okay?" Jack asks.

"I am freezing!" she replies feeling goosebumps all over her body.

Jack feels her head and it is like ice to touch.

"Well on that note peeps, we're going to leave that here for today! Come back tomorrow for our follow up on tonight's investigation!" Jack finishes and signs off with a wink.

Abi felt excitement come over her.

"Oh my god Ben! Can we try this? Not a Youtube video but have our own equipment and use the mirror! I have a singing bowl at home, we could use the mirror you saw Katrina in from the library. We might finally be able to find out if it is Katrina trying to contact us and why!"

She sat right on the edge of the sofa, hands together, fingers tapping each other excitedly.

"There's no talking you out of this is there?" he asked with a smile.

"Fine, but wait until tomorrow night. I can speak to Jack about how to do this all safely before we attempt anything."

Jumping up with exhilaration, she squeezed Ben tightly. "Thank you, thank you, thank you." She said and quickly kissed him on the cheek without thinking.

Chapter 8

Vibrant oranges and fiery reds filled the sky, as the sun began to set on a somewhat productive day.

"I should head home before it gets too dark and I trip over something again," Abi said to Ben, as she gathered her things together.
"I'll walk you to your door. I know you're only a few doors down but I'd rather know you got back okay." Ben offered.
"Oh aren't you the gentleman," Abi replied happily, butterflies fluttering in her stomach making her feel giddy.

They headed out into the summer evening air. Sun glowing on their skin as they walk towards Abi's home. Birds sang in the tall, leafy trees and a multicoloured hot air balloon hovered in the distance.

They pushed open the little wooden gate and walked up the uneven path and the steps to her front door.
"Thank you for walking me home. You know, I have a couple of steaks in the fridge if you'd like to stay for dinner. You've done so much for me today. It's the least I can do to thank you." She offered, playing with the keys in her hands.
"You know what? That sounds great." Ben replied, the look of lust in his eyes and a calm, charming smile.

Abi felt her heart rate race excitedly, knowing he would be with her for longer.

She popped her things down just inside the door and headed through to the kitchen, Ben following closely behind.

"I can't wait for this kitchen to be finished. I'm getting so bored living out of boxes." She complained as she fetched 2 plates, 2 glasses, cutlery and pans from the boxes on the floor.

"Glass of wine?" She offered, grabbing the bottle of White Zinfandel from the fridge along with a couple of steaks.

"Yes please," he replied. "Here, let me pour while you make a start on dinner."

She picked up the 2 thick, juicy steaks and popped them in the frying pan with some salt and pepper and some hand-cut chips into the oven, seasoned with salt, pepper and a little garlic.

In another pan, she had creamy peppercorn sauce thickening, ready to pour over the medium-rare steaks.

While they were waiting for the food to be cooked, Ben came up a little closer to Abi and handed her a glass of wine.

"Despite all the strange things that have happened today, I've really enjoyed spending time with you," Ben said to Abi, taking another step closer, her back against the counter.

"Yeah, me too." She said as she bit her lip, eyes down at the floor scared to meet his. Another step and they were face to face. He lifted her chin so they were looking straight at each other and tucked a stray hair behind her ear.

BANG!

Just as they were about to kiss, there was a huge bang from the room above them, making them both jump out of their skins and Abi dropping her glass of wine. It hit the ground sending a pinkish, reddish liquid and glass shards all over the floor.

Ben picked up the heavy, metal torch from under the sink and they both walked up the stairs, making sure to tread lightly as to not make the floorboards creak and bring attention to themselves.

"You did lock the back door after I reminded you this morning right?" He whispered, concerned that someone had got in whilst they were at his house.

"Yes.. of course I did." She replied, when actually she wasn't entirely sure and was now questioning herself in her head.

They got to the landing and saw Abi's bedroom door open slightly. They crept up and gently pushed the door open. Ben flashed the torch around the room before heading in to check if anyone was in there. With no one to be found he flicked the light switch, flooding the room with light.

As they stepped into the room they saw her dressing mirror on the floor. Abi bent down to pick it up. Luckily it hadn't broken. She popped it back on top of her dressing table and tapped around it and shook the table to see if it moved.

It does not.

She looked at Ben, her eyes wide with anxiety.
"Well that's strange!" Ben said, them both standing as still as statues listening for any other noises.
When nothing else happened they decided to return downstairs.

"The Steaks!" Abi called out, hoping dinner hadn't been ruined.

She ran down the stairs, as quickly as her legs would take her, slid across the kitchen tiles and grabbed the frying pan removing it from the heat.
Luckily, she had put the hob on low so when she removed the steaks, they were perfectly cooked. She served up onto plates and added her homemade chips and placed them on the table.
As Abi went back to the kitchen to grab the cutlery and the peppercorn sauce, Ben lit the candles on the table and placed the glasses of wine next to their plates.

Abi smiled warmly and sat down to eat.

"So how long has your friend been ghost hunting?" Abi asked.
"Roughly 10 years now," Ben replied. "He first started when he was 19. He went to the screaming woods in Pluckley with a friend of his who was hoping to get into the media industry. They had the most terrifying experience in those woods. They saw eyes through the trees so headed in that direction to see if they could find whatever it was. As they were walking they heard an ear-piercing scream and a white face came towards them and went straight through him!"
"Oh my god really?! I would have been terrified!" Abi replied.
"Yeah, tell me about it. After that, he invested in lots of fancy equipment, went to a different location every week and he's even done an episode over in America with Ryan and Aaron from 'The Ghost Escapades'".

"Wow, that's impressive! Well it would be great to get some tips from him for tomorrow night." Abi replied.

"Yeah, hopefully he's not too busy. I was wondering about asking him if his medium friend would have any tips too."

As they clinked glasses to toast to friendships and great ideas, the whole house fell into darkness and they felt a rush of cold air move past them blowing out the candles. Water started gushing from the old kitchen sink taps.

Abi sat glued to her seat, with her fingernails digging into the underneath of her chair, leaving Ben to go investigate.

He tried flicking the lights back on with no luck, then grabbed the torch from beside the stairs. Luckily he left it out from the last time. Ben headed into the kitchen and turned the taps. First to the left, then right. Nothing worked. They just wouldn't shut off.

He slid on the wet floor, reached under the sink and twisted the brass stopcock to shut off the supply. The water gradually stopped, leaving an annoying dripping noise.

"This is exactly what happened last night in the bathroom," Abi said, scared to her wits. "I could hear rushing water so I went into the hallway and saw it flowing from under the bathroom door. The bath was overflowing. I tried to turn the taps off, that's when I slipped and hit my head. I didn't have the chance to find the stopcock."

"I hate to sound forward but, would you like me to stay the night? I can sleep on the floor and if anything happens then I'm there with you so you don't get hurt again." Ben asked, He felt so protective over Abi.
He would feel just awful if anything were to happen to her, especially if he wasn't there to keep her safe.

"Are you sure? I mean, I would feel a lot better with someone here with me. I was so scared about staying here tonight on my own. I do have a blow-up mattress so you wouldn't have to sleep on the floor."
"Yeah that's fine! I feel better knowing you're safe." Ben replied.

Abi grabbed the candles and re-lit them.
Ben with the torch and Abi with the candles, started making their way up to the bedroom.

Abi set the candles up on the dressing table and lit the rest of the candles on her shelves. She was so pleased about her love of candles. "At least this addiction comes in handy!" she thought to herself.
She pulled out the bed and pump from the box and started blowing it up.

Abi thrust her foot up and down on the pump, wishing for the electric to come back on so she didn't have to continue to blow the bed up manually.
Ben looked around the room through her books and crystals, taking particular notice of the purple agate geode with its sparkly crystals in the centre.

A gust of wind swirls around them both, blowing out the candles. The air was ice cold and circled them like a tornado.

Abi was flung to the bed and everything fell silent. Not a sound to be heard. Then a soft whisper came from the dressing table, "Run."
And that is exactly what they did.

Ben grabbed Abi's hand and pulled her up and they ran as fast as they could, leaving everything behind.
As they were reaching for the front door, they heard a menacing cackle, as if someone found it so funny that they were running scared for their lives.

They got outside the house and the front door slammed behind them. They stopped to take a breath at the gate. Looking back at the house, all the lights suddenly switched on.

"No way are we going back in there until we have spoken to Jack. We can stay at mine." Ben said, holding her close.
She shakily whispered, "Okay." Not able to get any more than one word out.

Chapter 9

Proving himself the gentleman, Ben let Abi take the bed whilst he slept on the sticky leather sofa for the night.

His bedroom, again, was like a scene from a catalogue.
A shiny silver, four-poster bed with crisp, white sheets and black cushions.
White wooden drawers with piles of old but well-preserved adventure books and some limited additions.
A couple of small, spiky succulents dotted around on the few shelves and blackout curtains.
Why Ben hadn't redecorated in his own style, she would never know.

Despite the blackout curtains, Abi still woke at her usual time of 8 am. She saw Ben's dressing gown hanging on the back of the door and put it on over the top of her underwear.
It was massive, dark blue and felt like soft velvet which she just couldn't stop stroking.

She padded down the stairs quietly in case Ben wasn't awake yet.
"He must have had a terrible night on that god awful sofa." She thought to herself feeling a little guilty. She felt so bad for pulling him into this situation. She was, however, glad that she could turn to him. She didn't really have any other real friends. She had acquaintances but no one else she could really trust or turn to.

As she reached the last step, she could smell fresh, hot coffee beans.

"Oh just what I need." she thought as she rubbed her eyes.

Ben was up and in the kitchen pouring 2 cups of coffee, almost predicting her arrival.

"You must have read my mind." Abi greeted Ben in the arched doorway.

"Good morning, thought you might need it," Ben replied. After all the drama of the last couple of days and knowing there was more yet to come, he knew they both would need a good strong coffee to start their day.

"So plan for the day. I thought we could pay a visit to Jack. I sent him a message last night explaining what has been going on and he would love to meet you and talk to you about it. We might even be able to borrow some of his equipment if you're nice" Ben teased.

"I'm always nice!" she argued playfully back. "So did he mention a time at all?"

"He's free any time from 11 am. He works until 1 am and gets up at 9 am for a run. We will be meeting him at a cafe just around the corner from his studio for brunch."

"Oh well, I will definitely need to get changed then!" Abi said, with a hint of nerves at the thought of going back into her home without speaking to Jack first.

"Yes you will, but you'll not be stepping into that house this morning. We've got a couple of hours, we can pick you up some new clothes from the shops before we head to the cafe." Ben said, not really giving her an option, but she did feel some relief that she didn't have to go back in there yet.

Feeling a little grubby in yesterday's dungarees and t.shirt, she slips into the passenger seat of Ben's car. He must have got it valeted after the glass smashing incident the other day. The outside was gleaming with reflections from the sun and the interior was spotless and had that new car smell.

They drove out of their quiet neighbourhood and onto the busy dual carriageway that took them to the nearest shopping centre.

They pulled up outside a clothing boutique on a pretty town street, where each shop has a hanging basket of multi-coloured posies hanging outside the front door. Abi quickly popped into the boutique while Ben parked the car.

While Abi was in the dressing room trying on a long green cotton skirt and a white blouse, Ben handed the cashier his credit card details to pay the final amount of whatever the items came to and headed back to the car parked just outside.

Abi was surprised to learn that Ben had paid for her items and walked back out after changing in the shop, with yesterday's clothes in the boutique's designer paper bag.

"You really didn't have to do that Ben." She said, half annoyed with him and half thankful.

"Take it as a late birthday gift." He said with a smile, as he started to drive off in the direction of the cafe.

"You already got me a gift though, you got me those lovely flowers." She replied.

"Oh well, now you have something that will last. And you look lovely by the way." Ben complimented her.

"Thank you." She said, giving in with a small smile.

She popped her sunglasses on and relaxed a bit as they headed onto the bypass to the next town.

They pulled off the bypass at the next exit and within 5 minutes they were outside the cutest little cafe.

Purple wisteria clung to the white brickwork and surrounded the cottage-like door. Cute little white wooden tables and chairs sat out the front with sweet, potted flowers on each tabletop.

Jack sat waiting at one of the tables out the front, typing vigorously on his phone and a Spanish omelette in front of him.

"Hey ghost hunter," Ben called over as they walked up to the table.

"Hey Ben!" Jack said, putting his hand out to shake hands with him.

"And this must be the famous Abi! I've heard a lot about you." Jack said, shaking her hand as well.

"All good I hope." She said with a smile.

"Oh more than!" Jack replied. "I hear you've been renovating a Victorian house! That must be a lot of work?" Jack asked.

"Oh yes, quite! I have been working on It for a while now, but I'm almost finished now and with Ben's help these next few weeks it will be done in no time! He is quite the handyman." She replied.

"That's our Ben! The number of times he's helped me out of a sticky situation! I owe him big time. Which brings us to why we're meeting today. Ben tells me you're having a bit of a ghostly problem."

"That is a bit of an understatement," Abi replied with a quick giggle.

"Since my birthday, 2 days ago, I've heard voices, mirrors have smashed in my face or been knocked over, the taps keep coming to life and sending water everywhere. One night I ended up unconscious due to slipping in water from the overflowing tub and consequently hit my head. I've also been having very strange dreams about my ancestors. It's quite literally out of nowhere. I had never seen their photos until the afternoon of my birthday at my parent's house."

"That's not all." Ben interrupted, taking out the photo of Katrina.

"She also looks identical to this photo. The woman she has been dreaming about and whose reflection I saw in the mirror in her library."

"Wow. This is insane." Jack said in amazement looking at the photo.

A waitress, dressed head to toe in black and white maids clothing, came to take Ben and Abi's order. Ben decided on a bacon roll with a coffee and Abi chose scrambled egg on toast and a glass of apple juice. She couldn't understand how people could drink warm drinks when it's so unbelievably hot. Surely it must be the hottest day of the year so far.

"So, tonight we're wanting to see if we could get some answers on what is going on in Abi's house and we're hoping you may be able to give us some tips and ideas on how to do that. Obviously in a safe way too." Ben said to Jack.

"Okay, so before you do anything in the house, what we do first is stand in a circle holding each other's hands. Luna, my medium, will ask for the white light of protection to surround us and keep us safe throughout the night. She will ask for spirit guides to help guide us and protect us as we try to seek the truth and thank them for their guidance.

Step 2, she will ring her singing bowl to bring energy to the space.

After this, we will use the Ghost Box to try and capture any EVP's as we're asking questions.

Another experiment we've used in the past is the mirror experiment. You sit in front of the mirror and stare into your reflection. Many different things happened with this experiment. We've had the person's face change in the reflection, the person in the chair has noticed smelling different things or feeling different emotions. We've even had possessions and experienced the memories of the spirit." Ben explained informatively, taking a sip of ice tea.

"That's what I want to try. I have a mirror in the library, the one which Ben saw Katrina in. I want to try and use it to make contact with Katrina. I think that's how she communicates. We have both heard her voice coming from the mirror on my dressing table. It's like she's trying to warn us about something." Abi said as the waitress sets a glass of fresh, cold apple juice in front of her.

"Okay, so I have an idea for you. How about me and Luna come along tonight to help you out. I'd like to record any findings but if you don't want it going on to my channel then that's completely understandable. We can keep the findings to ourselves. Luna will be able to help with connecting to the spirits and providing protection and you will have full use of any equipment you wish to use."

"Okay," Abi said, having a little think. "I think I'd like to keep it away from public eyes for now. I need answers. I need to find out what's going on and why all this is happening. Maybe once we've gotten to the bottom of the investigation and we all get out of this safely then I'll think about letting it be shown, but for now, can we please just keep it between ourselves?" Abi asked.

"Of course, that's not a problem at all. How about we meet at the house at about 8 pm? We can get everything set up just before it gets dark and go from there?" Jack suggested.

"Sounds great!" Abi replied, excited to get started and finally get some answers. The only thing is, will they be the answers Abi is looking for?

Chapter 10

Just as it was coming up to 8 pm, a large black van with a large white logo of TGC in a circle pulled up. Under the logo, it read, 'Got a paranormal problem? Give The Ghost Catcher a call', followed by his phone number, website and Youtube channel.

Jack and Luna made their way down the crumbling footpath and up the wonky steps to Abi's front door.

Luna is a curvy, tall woman. Deep chocolate, wavy hair. Bright red lipstick on her perfectly pouty lips. She wore a black tank top with their business logo, revealing tattoos of black cats in witches hats and a triple moon representing the divine goddess, Maiden, Mother and Crone.

Abi felt an instant connection to Luna. The air surrounding her pulled Abi in like a big warm embrace with a sense of belonging.

"Hi! Welcome to my home." Abi said excitedly, giving both Jack and Luna a hug. "Sorry not all parts of the house are finished yet but there shouldn't be anything dangerous," she assured them.
"Not a problem," Jack replied. "So where's this library of yours?" Jack asked. And as if to answer his question, there is a loud bang from upstairs.
"In that direction I take it?" and they all started to laugh.

It could have been the nerves that made them laugh, but Abi was so glad they were there and it really gave her a boost in confidence.

They picked up bits of equipment each, Ben and Jack taking the heavier camera and sound equipment, while Abi and Luna took microphones, voice recorders and other small instruments.
Abi led the way up the old, creaky stairs onto the landing and through the tower door, up the steep spiral staircase.
The sunset beamed through the little arch window as they headed upwards.

Abi pushed open the heavy, oak, arched door and stepped into the newly carpeted library.

Whilst Ben and Abi waited for Jack and Luna to arrive earlier on, they emptied all of the cardboard boxes and filled the shelves with books and ornaments. At least now there was nothing on the floor for them to trip over or hurt themselves.
They all stepped into the stunning library. Any book lover would dream to have a library like this.

The golden framed mirror, a little tarnished around the edges, was set up on a table, leaning up against the wall with a dark blue, fabric armchair sitting with brown wooden feet in front of it.

Jack set up three cameras. One facing a side view of the chair and mirror and the other facing into the mirror to be able to catch any facial changes that may occur. The final camera is set up in the corner of the room so they can catch anything that happens around them.

Cameras all switched on ready, they all sat and waited for Jack to complete his equipment tests.

Faintly from behind the library door... bonk, bonk, bonk, bonk, bonk.
Footsteps came up the stairs and stopped as though they couldn't come any further. They all froze and stayed silent for what felt like minutes but really, it was just seconds.

BANG!

The door came crashing open, hitting the wall and slammed shut again.

Jack ran towards the door with his handheld camera and frantically twisted and turned the old brass doorknob but failed to open the door. He stood back away from the door but the handle kept twisting and turning on its own and the huge, heavy door started shaking.

Abi was standing behind Ben holding tightly onto his hand.

The shaking seemed to spread around the room. The paintings on the walls started to shake and fall to the ground, making its way around to the new bookshelves they had just put up yesterday and books started flying off of the many shelves.

Abi, Ben, Jack and Luna were now all huddled together in the middle of the room holding each other's hands and Luna asked for the other three to imagine a bright white protective light around them. As long as they had this protection, nothing could harm them. She asked for passed loved ones and spirit guides to come forward and help them through the night.
She finished with the words, "So mote it be!"

Everything stopped suddenly. No sounds. No movement. A deafening silence filled the room. Everyone's hearts were racing. Hairs all standing on end from the blast of energy in the room.

Abi then saw something written on the mirror. 'IT'S HER', it read on the foggy glass.
"Uh Jack... You might want to see this." Abi said as she headed closer to the mirror.
"Don't touch it!" He replied, focusing on the writing with his camera.
"I think it's time we did the mirror experiment Abi." He said.
Abi took in a big, deep breath, "Okay." She replied, trying to be brave.

She sat down in the comfy armchair. Shook out her arms and legs then settled. Looking down at her shoes she took some calming, slow breaths. In... and out. In... and out.
Luna then picked up her singing bowl and tapped it on the side letting out a loud ringing noise and circled it to create a soothing effect.
Once the beautiful sound finished, Abi lifted her head to face the mirror and opened her eyes.

She stared in silence at her reflection. She heard a ticking in the background, although she had no clocks. Her clothes started to change and she was now sitting wearing a long white nightgown.

Out of shock, she turned around and said "Guys are you seeing this?!" but to her surprise, there was no one there. She turned back to look at her reflection and it's now daytime.

She got up from the chair and walked over to the bed feeling light-headed.
She climbed into the wooden framed bed. The duvet smelled like mothballs.
As she laid back in the bed, a woman walked into the bedroom holding a tray in her hands which held a glass of milk and a hot bowl of vegetable broth.
"Thank you, Helen," Abi replied. "How the hell did I know her name?!" She thought to herself.
"You're welcome Mrs Taylor Ma'am," Helen replied.
"WHAT?!" She thought. This couldn't be happening.
She couldn't control her actions. Abi, or should we say, Katrina, lifted the old silver spoon with an ornate handle and dipped it into the soup and brought it to her lips to take a sip. It had a chemical taste to it but she couldn't stop eating the soup. Still sitting in the bed, she got a small tickly cough. The cough got stronger and it became hard to breathe. She started choking and fell out of the bed onto the floor.

Ben, Jack and Luna surround her as she wakes up, laying on the soft blue carpet. As she woke, Abi realised the bedroom from her vision had looked like her actual present-day bedroom and it gave her chills.
Was that her bedroom?

She told the others what happened while she was out.

"Was Katrina poisoned?!" Ben suggested, helping Abi back onto the chair.
"Possibly. Whatever was in that soup certainly didn't taste nice. Or she just had a really bad cold and the nanny was just bringing her some lunch to make her feel better. We're still no closer to getting any answers, we've just had more bizarre activity." Abi said.

"Why don't we try the spirit box?" Jack suggested picking up a black, cylinder-shaped piece of equipment.
All in agreement, Jack switched the spirit box on. It rapidly flicked through sounds of white noise. Foosh, foosh, foosh, foosh, foosh.
They all stand close hoping that something would come through and they don't miss it.

"Abi, I think you should call out to Katrina. I believe she has a connection to you. You've dreamt of her and shared her memories. I think if she were to speak to anyone, it would be you." Luna suggested.

"Okay, I'll give it a go," Abi said, nerves kicking in after what she has already gone through with the mirror experiment.

Ben heard the nerves in her voice and reached out to hold her hand.

"It's okay." He reassured her.

Abi took a deep breath and called out.

"Katrina are you here?"

They waited for a reply but heard only the white noise.

"Katrina, please, if you have a message or need help then let us know. Give us a sign."

They heard what sounds like a baby cry.

"Did you hear that?!" Abi said, grabbing Ben's arm with her free hand.

They all replied in unison. "YES!"

"Keep going Abi," said Jack.

"Katrina, how did you die?" Abi asked, feeling sick as soon as she did.

They waited for an answer to come through in the white noise.

"Water." said a woman's voice.

"Did she just say water?!" Abi asked, sounding completely shocked.

"Maybe that's why the taps keep turning on. Water."

The paintings started shaking on the wall.

Abi called out "Katrina is that you? What's happening?"

Out of the white noise came another voice "Mine!"

"Who are you? What is yours?" Abi shouted out as the shaking got louder.

"He is." The voice replied.

"Who is he? Who is yours?" Abi asked.

All of the equipment shut off. It's as if all the batteries had been completely drained. Even the heavy-duty torch wouldn't switch on. They were left in complete darkness and a stench of ammonia filled the room.

"Oh my god! What is that smell? Tell me everyone else can smell that too?!" Ben said, covering his nose and mouth with his hand.

49

"Oh it's gross!" Said Abi, letting go of Ben's hand and also covered her face. "Something bad is here. It's not Katrina." Said Luna sounding as freaked out as the rest of them. "Bad, evil entities give off an ammonia-like smell," Luna informed them.

As quick as the smell came, it went. As if being sucked away by an invisible vacuum. "Well that was weird." Said Abi, now feeling a bit light-headed, she sat down in the armchair and the lights flickered back on.

While the room's energy seemed to have settled, Jack started listening back on the voice recorder to see if they captured any EVP's. He wandered over to the bookcase and leaned against it while listening to the recording through his headphones.

Abi looked at the books on the floor that had been thrown from the bookcase earlier when they first started investigating.

The Water Knife.
A Long Walk To Water.
Memory Of Water.
Water For Elephants.
Down River.

All of these books had one, very clear thing in common. WATER. Abi bent down picking up all the books and piled them up on the table after realising the common quality.

"Look at the books!" Abi said to Ben and Luna. "They're all to do with water!" She said excitedly after stumbling upon the clue left behind.
"That's crazy!" Ben replied.
"So we have the water from the bath on the night of my birthday, the kitchen taps coming on the following day and now the books... all to do with water," Abi says.
"Do you think maybe she drowned in the bath?" Ben suggested.
"I feel that water and drowning are definitely relevant but I don't feel as though it was in the bath. I feel it was away from here." Luna replied with both hands placed gently on top of the recently fallen books.

"Oh my god! Do you think that woman killed Katrina? The voice that was saying "He's mine" like she was jealous of Katrina." Abi questioned.
"Oh maybe!" Ben replied thinking Abi may be on to something.

"We're going to need more evidence though. These are just ideas." Abi said, realising that they need more to go on.

"Hey guys, you need to listen to this," Jack said, pulling the headphone out so that the recording can be heard by everyone.
"This was recorded while you were in a trance state during the mirror experiment," Jack explained.

He clicked play.

A blood-curdling cry came from the small device, then a woman's voice cried out "Henry!"

As soon as Abi heard the voice saying Henry, she felt pin pricks in her eyes as they started to fill with tears.

"Henry was the name of Katrina's son!" Abi proclaimed in disbelief to what she was hearing.
"Have you come across any information on her baby Abi?" Asked Ben.
"No, I didn't think to look for anything on him. I'll have to do some more research once we're done tonight." She said.
"We heard a baby cry when we turned on the spirit box, didn't we? I didn't imagine that, did I?" Ben asked.
"We definitely heard that!" Jack replied quickly.
"Oh, you don't think Henry died as a baby do you?" Abi asked Ben, sounding sad.
"I hope not, but it would make sense to link it together like that wouldn't it?" He asked.
"I suppose so. I have to find some more information on them. And I want to find out who that woman's voice belonged to as well." Abi replied.
"Agreed." Said Ben. "We can head over to mine again for the night. No way on earth am I letting you stay in the house alone now. Then in the morning we can start doing some more research on Katrina and her family."
"Thanks Ben." Abi agreed.

"Let's call this a wrap for tonight then," Ben said, as he spoke into his voice recorder. "Investigation ends at 3.30 am".
"We can meet back here tomorrow to catch up and go over anything you may find?" Jack suggested.

"Yeah definitely," Abi replied in agreement. "Shall we say 5 pm? I can do dinner for us all. I have the carpenter coming to fit my cabinets tomorrow so the kitchen will be finished by the time you get here."

"Sounds great," Jack commented as they started to gather up the equipment.

Chapter 11

Abi woke up the next morning in Ben's four-poster bed. She rolled over and checked the time. 9 am.
"Crap!" She cried out loud in a panic, remembering that the carpenter would be around this morning to fit the kitchen cabinets for her.
She jumped out of bed and got dressed as quickly as she could, tripping over whilst putting on her shorts.

THUD.

Ben was in the kitchen making coffees when he heard the thud above him. He filled a mug with steamy, hot coffee and headed upstairs to check on Abi.

He lightly tapped on the door. "Are you decent?" Ben called through the door.

"Yep!" Abi replied, as she quickly struggled to zip up her shorts whilst still laying on the floor by the bed.

Ben walked in and saw Abi's head on the floor by the end of the bed. "Well hello head." Ben greeted her trying not to laugh but with a smile on his face.
"Hi." She said back. "Sorry about the noise, I'm in a hurry. The carpenter is going to be here any minute and I'm not home!" She said, panicking.

The Woman In The Mirror

"Oh right, grab your bag and I'll bring the coffees with us. May as well start that research together whilst the handyman fits your kitchen." Said Ben.

She grabbed her stuff and they both hurried down the stairs and out the front door.

Just as they reached the gate to Abi's house, a van pulled up.
"Well, that was good timing!" Abi said, relieved that they got there just in time.

Abi showed the carpenter into the kitchen whilst Ben went into the living room, out of the way.
She let the carpenter know what she wanted and where, then left him to get on with his job and popped a cup of coffee on the side for him before joining Ben in the living room.

She handed Ben the Laptop so he could plug in his dongle.
"I'm just going to pop to the loo if you want to get the laptop fired up," she said to Ben.

"Yep that's fine. I've got the dongle so the speed won't be as fast as usual but i'll get started!" He replied.

Abi walked up the stairs and along the hallway to the bathroom. After she finished she washed her hands and turned the tap off.
She dried her hands on the white, fluffy, Egyptian cotton towels, warm from the heated towel rail.

"Abi." A soft voice whispered behind her. She jumped and turned to face the mirror.
"Abi." She heard again whilst looking at herself in the mirror.
She walked slowly up to the mirror and gently placed her hand on the mirror, palm flat to the cold glass.
Within seconds she dropped to the floor.

Standing outside the house, she opened the old white gate and walked up the neat, tidy path and up the painted steps to her front door. Something didn't seem right.
She heard arguing from inside the house but couldn't make out the words.
She turned the handle and stepped into the house.
Stomping furiously down the stairs came James, the look of rage across his face.
"Is everything okay darling?" Katrina asked her husband.

"Everything is fine dear," James replied very unconvincingly.
"I'll go check on Henry," Katrina said.

Her laced gloved hand settled on the wooden bannister and floated gracefully up the stairs as if trained for a beauty pageant. She reached the landing then headed towards the baby's nursery.
She opened the door and saw Helen, the nanny, with a small vial of clear liquid in one hand and the baby's milk bottle in her other. She started to pour.
Katrina stormed in running towards Helen screaming "Stay away from my baby!". She pushed Helen to the floor and grabbed her by the throat, slowly squeezing and shouted "You're trying to kill my baby!"
James came running in.
He grabbed Katrina by her arms tightly and pulled her away, releasing Katrina's hands from Helens now red, sore throat.
"She's trying to kill our baby! She is trying to kill Henry!" She screamed and shouted in a frenzy, being dragged onto the landing by James.

Helen crawled forward on her knees and pulled herself up the set of drawers and quickly swapped out the bottle of milk for a fresh one without any other liquids added.
James managed to get Katrina down the stairs and out to the carriage, Katrina screamed all the way, "Why won't you believe me? Why won't you listen?! This is the third time I've caught her and you never believe me!"
"You'll calm down and see sense soon my love. It's your imagination again. Helen was just feeding our son, that is all. Just like last time. We will go for a drive for you to calm down. Drink this and you'll be thinking straight again soon. You just need some air." He said, handing her his whiskey flask. He stood and whispered in the coachman's ear where to take them.
Katrina seemed to pass out.

The visions dim out and back in.

They now stand by the steps of a large, hospital-like building. A yellow stock brick building with octagonal towers and an ornate clock face in a wooden setting at the top of the middle tower.

Katrina held onto James' arm, still not with it and walked in a zombie-like state up to the building's arched doorway.

They stepped inside, where a lady in a nurse's uniform greets them.

James sat Katrina down in a chair. She stayed in her own little world.

James spoke to the head nurse away from Katrina, yet she still heard him but didn't have the energy to do anything.

He explained to the nurse that his wife had been gradually going insane, imagining things and has now become a danger to himself, baby and nanny. He told her how he just had to drag her away from the nanny before she killed her.

The nurse agreed to take her on and took payment for treatment for the next 3 months.

He walked back over to Katrina. He told her that everything is going to be alright. These people were going to help her get better and that he would be back to get her once she had recovered.

Katrina tried to talk but not a word came out of her mouth. She couldn't even move her lips.

"Goodbye, darling," James said to Katrina, leaving a kiss on her cheek as he left.

The head nurse walked over to Katrina. "Come on then hunnie, let's get you settled in." She said to Katrina, placing her hand on Katrina's arm.

Feeling a surge of energy, Katrina stood straight up, pulled her arm away from the nurse and shouted at the top of her lungs, "Nooo!"

Abi woke up on the floor, Ben banging on the door shouting "Abi?! Abi, are you okay?"

He shouted through the door, banging aggressively.

Abi sat up, reached the lock and turned it to the right and it clicked.

Ben opened the door to Abi sitting on the floor with her head in her hands.

"Abi what happened? Are you okay?" He asked worryingly.

"I think I'm okay. I think I had another vision. Katrina was in the Asylum." She announced, feeling completely drained.

"That's just what I was wanting to talk to you about." Not surprised at what Abi had just told him.

He helped Abi up and they walked downstairs into the living room. He sat Abi down and passed her a glass of water.

"Look what I found." Ben insisted, excited at his discovery.

On the laptop screen was a document.
It read:

Blue Waters Patient Registration

"Ben! How did you find this?!" She questioned in amazement.
"It was hard to find but I went through a lot of different government pages and hospital documents," Ben explained.
"Keep reading further down." He said.

Blue Waters Patient Registration

Patient name: Katrina Taylor
Next of Kin - James Taylor
Reason for registration - Danger to self and others. Hallucinations. Delusional. Erratic Episodes.
Treatment- Hydro-Therapy
Date of arrival- 15.SEP.1859
Date of release- 15.DEC.1859
Printed - Head Nurse Margaret Davies
Signed - M. A. Davies

"This confirms it!" Abi proclaimed. "This explains the vision I just had! That could mean my other visions and dreams were real too!" she said, feeling reassured by the evidence Ben had found.

She grabbed her notepad and a pen. She drew out a grid and started to write down her visions in one column and evidence in the other column.

Visions	Evidence
Dreamt I was by a river in Victorian dress, a shadow comes towards me and I scream and wake up	Spirit box revealed that Katrina possibly died in water - could this be the river from my dream but no physical evidence yet!
Dreamt of the day Katrina met James then turned into rushing water	
Vision in the mirror - being in bed and Helen brings soup and milk and I start coughing	Helen was the nanny - evidence from article on Katrina's disappearance
Vision of Helen pouring a liquid into Henry's milk bottle, Katrina tackling her to the floor then ending up in the Asylum	Blue water Asylum records showing date of admission and release of Katrina

"Great Idea Abi." Ben said. "I'm going to try and do a search on this Helen Watson and see if I can get any info on her."
"Brilliant. I'm just going to check on the carpenter and see how it's going, back in a sec." Abi replied, popping her notepad and pen back on the coffee table.

Ben typed into the search engine, Helen Watson 1850's, and clicked search.

Helen Watson Genealogy 1950s

Date of birth- 14 May 1836.
Date of Death - 16 Sep 1861.
Age upon death - 25 yrs
Never married.
Had no children.

Daughter of John Watson and Mary Watson.
Only child.
Number of workplaces - One
Employer - James and Katrina Taylor
Dates worked for previous employer - 1859-1861
Job Role - Nanny

Click here for more info

Ben clicked the more info button.

Helen Watson is reported missing by her employer James Taylor. Her suspicious disappearance came 1 year before the kidnapping of Mr Taylor's baby boy Henry. After the kidnapping of poor Henry, Helen Watson became the housekeeper so that James could keep her in employment.
Mr Taylor seems to have been dealt a hand of bad luck as this would now become the 3rd disappearance within the household.
Mr Taylor's wife, Katrina Taylor, went missing on 30th April 1860 and was reported 1 day later on the 1st May 1860.
Mr Taylor, feeling his bad luck was linked to the house, put his property, located on England road (now presently known as Old England road), on the market.

Below this article from 2016, were some black and white photos.

The first photo was of Helen Watson.
She had blond curly hair, pinned at the top of her head, wearing her housemaid uniform.
The 2nd photo was of James Taylor, dressed in his Sunday best, standing next to a fireplace.

The 3rd photo is the one that gave Ben the chills and made his stomach start turning.
It was a photo of the home that James had put up for sale.
Abi's house!

"Uh, Abi!" Ben called through to the kitchen. "I think I've found something you might want to see.

"Please excuse me." Abi apologised to the carpenter, who had done a pretty good job so far and was already halfway done.
"What did you find?" She asked.

Ben turned the laptop round to show Abi the photo on the screen.

As soon as she saw it, all the colour from her face seemed to disappear and she ran to the bathroom to be sick.

Ben rushed into the kitchen to grab a fresh glass of water. "Sorry mate," He said to the carpenter. "There's been a lot of weird things going on here at the moment." He commented as he filled up a glass.

"Not at all." The carpenter replied. "I've known a lot of strange things to happen in homes like this."

Ben turned around to face him and take the water to Abi. He looked straight into the carpenter's eyes and was in shock.
It's the same face as the man who was just on his laptop screen.
"Excuse me," Ben says as he passes the carpenter.

He ran up the stairs with a glass of water to Abi who was just coming out of the bathroom.
He grabbed her and pulled her into her bedroom and shut the door quietly behind him and pressed his ear against it to listen for any noises.
Happy that they're alone, he turned to Abi and said quietly, "The man downstairs... He looks just like James! He is identical to the photo that was on my screen just a few minutes ago!" He exclaimed.
"No, That can be." She replied, "I need to look at the photo again."

They head back downstairs quietly and look at the photo of James on the laptop. Every detail right down to the curly moustache! He was right.

The home is strangely quiet for a house that had work being done in the kitchen. They both stand up and walk towards the kitchen.
The carpenter had vanished. All the cabinets were still on the floor waiting to be put up, even though Abi had been in to check on him and it had looked to be nearly complete.

"What the hell!" she said, completely confused.

They both looked out the window and the van was gone too.

She pulled her phone out, called the company that sent the carpenter and put it on the loudspeaker.

"Hi I need to speak to someone about the carpenter attending my property today." She requested the man on the other end.
"That's fine, can I take your name and first line of address please?" The man asked.
"It's Abi Howard, 213 Old England Road." She replied.
The man tapped away on his computer.
"Oh yes. I can see here that the engineer is running late but should be with you in.. 10 minutes" He said after checking notes and location of the van.
"But he's already been and after 3 hours of work he's disappeared and all the cabinets are back on the floor as if no work had been done at all," Abi complained.
"Oh I am sorry, but that wouldn't have been one of ours. I'm looking at the van tracker now and he is driving in your direction and should be there any minute." He explained.
"Okay thank you," Abi replied, putting the phone down, feeling even sicker than before.

"That doesn't make any sense at all!" Ben says. "James wasn't even a carpenter was he? I thought he was a painter?" Ben questioned.
"That's what I thought too." Abi agreed.

Chapter 12

It's 4 pm and the carpenter is packing his tools away. Luckily this time there was no silly business and the kitchen looked great.

Ben started helping Abi unpack the boxes full of plates, bowls, glasses, mugs and all the other usual kitchen utensils and put them away in their new homes.
It now felt complete and Abi was over the moon with how her kitchen now looked. She took two glasses from the top cupboard and a cold bottle of Prosecco from the fridge. She set the glasses down and poured the golden liquid, being careful to not let it bubble over.

She handed one glass to Ben and they toasted to finding answers and finishing homes.
"So, fancy anything in particular for dinner?" She asked Ben. "I have no idea what Jack and Luna would like."
"How about, save on cooking, let's just get Chinese. Everyone loves Chinese! I can send a message to Jack and see what they would like to order and we can have it here in time for when they turn up." Ben suggested, with his phone in his hand.
"Yeah go on then." Abi agreed, quite happy she didn't have to cook.

Ben typed out a quick message to Jack and he replied instantly.

While Abi placed the order, Ben got plates and cutlery and set the table, ready for when the food arrived.

Abi and Ben tried to squeeze in a little more research.

This time they searched for baby Henry. In the last research they found on Helen Watson, it said that she had gone missing a year after baby Henry had been kidnapped.

Abi typed in, 'Henry Taylor goes missing 1860' and hit search.

Sir Henry Taylor Portrait 1863

Lucy Taylor - where is she

John Taylor Genealogy

"I'm not having any luck," Abi complained to Ben.

Ben on the other hand stumbled across another article.

20-Jul-1860

Almost 3 months after the disappearance of Katrina Taylor, her son Henry Taylor is now also reported missing.
Katrina Taylor was reported missing on 1st May and investigators have still not found her!
Is she still alive? And if so, did she come back for her 14-month-old son Henry?
Police are urging anyone with any information to please come forward.
A cash reward is also available for the safe return of Henry Taylor to his father James Taylor of 213 England Road.

A little further down is another link which he clicks.

Did the maid do it?

The link took him to what looked like an article from a gossip panel in a newspaper.

Did the maid do it?

Many speculate that the maid is behind the disappearances of Katrina and Henry Taylor.

When Mr Taylor was questioned by detectives at his home back in July last year, Miss Watson was very overprotective of Mr Taylor. She stood behind him, her hand on his shoulder.

She had to be removed from the room as a result of continuous interruptions whilst questioning Mr Taylor.

When detectives questioned why she was so protective of Mr Taylor, she would reply explaining how he had been through a lot already in the last year with the disappearance of his wife and now his baby being kidnapped.

As Ben was reading this, the electrics went berserk.

The lights flashed on and off, the radio flicked through all the different stations with weird noises and screams coming from it. All of the dining room chairs were thrown into the air, including the one Ben was sitting on, leaving him now on the floor after hitting his head on the table. And with a high pitched pop, all the electrics blew and they were left in an energy-charged silence.

Abi was on the kitchen floor, hands over her head to protect her from anything that might hit her and Ben on the dining room floor in the fetal position.

Feeling the silence all around them, they relaxed, well tried to.
"I'm getting sick of this," Abi complained. "Are you okay Ben?" She asked, still shaking.
"Yeah, I just hit my head on the table after being thrown from my chair, but I'm okay," he said, heart still racing.

Then 3 big bangs.

"Oh for god's sake," Abi said, feeling as though she was about to have a heart attack.
"It's just the Chinese." She explained. "I need to get a doorbell."
Hand on his heart after jumping at the bangs, "Yes, yes you do!" Ben said, shaking his head.

Abi opened the door and took in the takeaway. As she did so, Jack and Luna were making their way down the path as well.

"Oh thank god you're here." She said hugging them both, still with the bag of Chinese in her hand.
"Whoa, what happened here?" Jack questioned, noticing the chairs flung all over the place, plants knocked over and cutlery all over the floor in the kitchen.

"You just missed the biggest surge of activity we've had so far," Ben said, rubbing his sore head.

"What happened to you?" Jack asked, looking at Ben.

"Oh nothing much, just got thrown from my chair and hit my head on the table."

"What?! Are you serious?" Jack questioned.

Moving his hand away from his head, Ben showed a big purple bruise on his forehead.

"Ouch!" Jack replied, when he saw how big the bruise on his friend's head was.

"Well, let's hope that wasn't all of the activity for this evening!" Jack said.

Abi started picking the chairs up and re-laid the table so they could sit down and eat while they discussed any findings they found during their research.

She placed all the boxes on the table and removed the lids to reveal steamy, hot food that filled the air with a mouth-watering aroma.

She sat down to join the rest of the group and they all helped themselves to the pick and mix of Chinese food that lay before them.

"So, any luck on the research?" Jack asked them both, as he leaned over to get some satay chicken.

"Mmmmm, Yes," Ben said, finishing his mouthful of egg fried rice.

"So, it turns out, Katrina had been admitted to Blue Waters Asylum. Her husband believed she was going crazy and her attack on the nanny was the last straw it seems."

"Wait. Hold up. Katrina attacked the nanny? I thought Katrina was the good guy in this story?" Jack questioned.

"I still believe she is." Said Ben confidently.

"I also found a couple of articles on Helen Watson, the nanny. The first was an article about her going missing."

"The nanny went missing too?! Are we sure James didn't just kill them both off?" Jack asked.

"I don't think so."Ben went on to explain, "She goes missing around a year after baby Henry does and I can't understand why he would want his baby dead too."

"Oh, I didn't know the baby was gone too!" Jack sympathised.

"That's not all," Abi informed him.

"We also found out that after all this bad luck, James put his house up for sale. His house being this house!"

"You're kidding right?" Jack said, almost choking on a chicken ball.

"Well that would explain why you felt so drawn into buying this house Abi. You have a strong connection with it and the souls that remain here," explained Luna, lining up her cutlery on her plate as she finished her food.

Noticing everyone had finished with their dinner, Abi collected up the empty plates and cutlery and took them out into the kitchen. She popped it all in the dishwasher, grabbed a jug of water and rejoined the group in the dining room.
She poured everyone a drink whilst Ben showed them the articles they had come across and the graph Abi had started writing up.

Again, when Ben got to the story about Helen and how overprotective she was with James while interviews were going on, the lights started flickering.

"Well, I think that's our cue to get investigating," Jack suggested.
"Why don't we try the mirror experiment again after last time's success?" Jack asked as he stood to get the equipment from his van.
"Sure," Abi replied as Jack headed to the door.

Tonight they decided to investigate in a different room, Abi's bedroom.

They headed up the stairs with as much equipment as they could carry.
They got set up in her bedroom.
Abi positioned herself in front of her dressing table mirror and sat on one of the dining room chairs rather than her stool. At least this way she would have back support in case she were to have another vision.

Luna had already asked for protection and finished her ritual with the sounds from her singing bowl.

Just as before, Abi raised her head and looked into the mirror. Her reflection stared back at her.

The camera set up over Abi's shoulder captured a fascinating change in Abi's facial appearance!
"Guys..."Abi said with fear in her voice. "What's going on?"
She continued to stare straight into her own eyes, but at this point, they didn't look like her own eyes.

Staring back at her was a different woman.
Not Katrina.

This lady had blond curly hair, but her hair looks muddy and messy. She has blue eyes that seemed to hold all the anger in the world as they glared back at Abi. "He's mine." She whispered.

But the voice didn't come from the mirror, it came from the spirit box as if she couldn't muster up enough energy to have her voice heard through the mirror.

Abi felt the anger come through from the mirror and confronted the woman.

"Is that all you can do? All you can say? You're nothing!" Abi shouted at the mirror.

The reflection started laughing. An evil long cackle. Then stopped dead and her hand reached up and started coming towards Abi in the mirror.

Everyone gobsmacked and in shock, saw a transparent arm reach out of the mirror and touch Abi's forehead.

Abi's head dropped forward.

She was in the garden. Beautiful, colourful flowers lined the fencing of the back garden. A pond sparkled in the sunlight at the end of the garden.

She heard giggling and laughing from inside the house. A woman and a man's voice she heard.

She headed inside. She saw no one downstairs so she started making her way up the staircase.

She headed past the nursery where she saw Henry in his crib and continued to her bedroom. Katrina's bedroom.

The door was wide open, so Abi could see everything.

James was sitting on the edge of the bed, his top 3 buttons undone on his shirt, revealing the black hair that coated his chest.

Leaning in and kissing him... the nanny.

The blond curly hair of the maid triggered something in Abi's brain.

The woman in the mirror was the nanny.

She could not believe what she was seeing and rushed up to them.

She reached forward to grab the nanny but her arms fell straight through her. Abi wasn't really there. She couldn't touch, pick up or move anything.

The nanny continues to giggle and out of nowhere says, "Is that all you can do?" Mimicking Abi as she pushed James back onto the bed and climbed on top of him, taking the pins from her hair to let it flow over her shoulders.

"Stop!" Abi screamed as she closed her eyes.

When Abi re-opened her eyes, she was back in her bedroom. Not Katrina's. Hers. She looked back in the mirror and Helen was still there, staring right back at her and laughing.

Not being able to take any more of her laughing, Abi clenched her hand into a fist and punched the mirror right where Helen's face was, sending glass everywhere and cutting her knuckles.

"Abi! What are you doing?" Ben shouted, taking her hand in his and checking for glass splinters.
"Guys, please keep an eye on Abi. I'm going to grab the first aid box from the kitchen." Ben said.

Just as he was about to go out the door, it slammed in his face, stopping him from leaving. "Erm Abi, I think you angered Helen." He suggested to her.
"Uh no... she was already angry," Abi replied.

The door handle started shaking as if someone was trying to open it.
Luna's head flung backwards. "He's mine!" A voice not belonging to Luna came out of her mouth.
"Yeah, yeah. We get it. You want James." Abi said.
"You cannot have him." The voice growled in anger.
Luna's body lurched towards Ben and the door suddenly opened. He ran through the door and into the bathroom locking himself in.
"You think you can get away from me?" She laughed.

The bath taps sprung to life, filling the bath with water. The sink taps then followed suit two seconds later. He unlocked the door and went to open it, planning on pushing Luna's body out of the way. Instead, once he unlocked the door, the door wouldn't open.
All he heard was Helens laugh coming from Luna's body.

Abi and Jack tried pulling her away from the door.
Luna's arms swung out sending both Abi and Jack flying into the walls along the hallway.

"Abi! Jack!" Ben called from inside the bathroom. The water from the sink and bath was overflowing onto the floor. For some strange reason, the water wasn't flowing underneath the door!

Instead, the bathroom started filling up like a swimming pool, as if someone had sealed the gap under the door and made it watertight.

"The bathroom is filling with water! I'm going to drown if you don't stop her!" Ben shouted out, terrified.

"We're trying!" Jack shouted back.

"Luna! Remember who you are. We know you're in there. Don't let Helen do this!" Abi begged, hoping to somehow get through to Luna.

"Luna, listen to Abi. This isn't you. You're kind. You help people. Listen to your guides, they will help you. Come back to me, Luna!" Jack shouted.

"Guys, it's getting bad! My feet are off the ground!" Ben now had to stay afloat until there was no more room to breathe.

Helen laughed even harder knowing Ben's time was almost up.

"Helpppp!" Ben shouted, now desperate for his life. The water was just centimetres from the ceiling and rising.

Taking one last deep breath, Ben's head went under the water.

Jack ran up to Luna. "This is not how I wanted this to happen." He said looking her in the eyes.

He kissed her.

Luna's eyes started to close hesitantly and Helen was finally gone.

The door slammed open and all the water came gushing out, Ben being slammed into the wall opposite by the force of the water.

He started coughing and spluttering, but he was alive.

Abi rushed over to him and put her arms around him.

"I'm so glad you're alive!" She said, Tears in her eyes, she kissed him. She pulled away quickly. "I'm sorry."

"Nope." He replied. He took her face in his hands and kissed her passionately.

Chapter 13

It was 4am and Abi was lying fast asleep, her arm wrapped around Ben's warm, unclothed body.

She slept deeply.

Feeling a strong magnetic pull, Abi sat up, eyes still fastened tightly shut. She walked slowly out of the dark bedroom and down the stairs, as if something was guiding her in her sleep, one slow step at a time.
She reached the bottom of the stairs, walked out the front door leaving it wide open, down the garden path and out onto the lamp-lit street.

She walked along the main road, a few cars making their way to work for their early shifts and others coming home from night shifts, but not one of them stopped when they saw the woman in a white nightdress walking along the road in the early hours of the morning.

She continued to walk as the sun started to rise and walked so far that she ended up down the lane where she used to go as a teen. Her 'Safe place'.
The fence was no longer there, giving free access to the field and the windy stream.

She walked over the small bridge and down to the stream.
Abi stepped into flowing water and walked following the current of the stream and under the small stone bridge.

On the other side of the bridge, there is the smallest of waterfalls, only about 1 metre in height that falls into a dangerous, deep pool of water before narrowing into another stream.

As she got to the edge of the stream under the bridge, just as it fell into the deep pool below, a man walking his dog saw Abi as he was coming across the fields.
"Wait!" He shouted over to her, completely unaware that she was sleepwalking.
"Hey lady!" He continued to shout.
Abi stood there as still as stone, oblivious to the fact that someone was calling after her.
Just as she was about to step off the edge, the stranger pulled her backwards, them both falling into the stream and she abruptly awoke, in shock and bewildered.

Meanwhile, back at the house, Ben woke up to find Abi not in bed. He got up and checked around the house. Abi was nowhere to be found.
He went back upstairs and got dressed. He pulled on a pair of jeans and a plain white t.shirt.
He went downstairs and headed to Abi's house thinking she must have popped back to hers.
He grabbed the spare key from under the heavy, blue plant pot outside the front door and headed into the house.

"Abi?!" He called out.
With no answer, he searched around the house.
In the bedroom the mirror was back on the floor, so he picked it back up and placed it back on her dressing table.
He then proceeded to go up into the library.
As he stepped into the library, sunrise light poured in from the big bay windows, he found books on the floor and paintings askew on the walls. The mirror that they had used for their investigations laid flat on the floor facing down.
He stood the mirror upright and noticed some words written in a fog on the glass.
'Her safe place.' It read.

The clue clicked in his head, he ran out the door and headed to his car.
Putting on his seat belt and shifting into first gear, he sped away, tyres screeching on the tarmac.
He put his foot down speeding around the corner and hurrying towards the country lane where he used to accompany Abi.

He pulled up next to the muddy lane slamming on his brakes. He jumped up out of his car, slammed the door behind him, not even bothering to make sure it had locked.

He ran down the lane, sliding through the mud as he went down the steep hill. As he reached the old bridge he saw Abi and a man in the stream.

He stumbled down the bank to the stream and helped them both up.

"What happened? Are you both okay?" Ben asked, relieved to find her safe.

"She was about to jump. I tried calling after her but she couldn't hear me. It was as if she was in a trance, I had to pull her back." The old man explained.

Abi sat in silence on the bank rocking backwards and forwards.

"Thank you so much for stopping her. She's been through a lot the last couple of days. I need to get her home. I'm parked just at the top of the hill, would you like a lift home? You must be freezing?" Ben offered.

"That would be brilliant, thank you." The man replied gratefully.

They got up to the car and Ben got the green patchwork blankets out of the boot. He handed one to the man who helped Abi and wrapped the other around her hoping to keep her warm.

"Don't worry about getting the seats wet and muddy, I need to get it in for a clean anyway," Ben assured him.

The old man thanked him and smiled. He slid onto the back seat and his small Jack Russell jumped on his lap.

Ben sat Abi down in the front seat with the blanket wrapped around her and buckled her in.

"Is she going to be okay?" Asked the old man out of concern for the lady he had just stopped from jumping to her death.

"I'm sure she will be fine. I'll get her home, run a warm bath and hopefully, she will start to relax. It looks as though she is in shock, sometimes it takes a while to come out of it." Ben explained, as he started to drive in the direction of the mans home.

"If you take the next turn and pull up by the post box, I'll jump out there." The man requested.

Ben took the left turn and slowed to a stop just before the small, red post box on the left.

A big Tudor style home with beautiful beams sat just back from the path.

"Thank you for the lift." He said to Ben. "I hope your girlfriend is feeling better soon."

"Thank you again for saving Abi today. I don't know what I would have done if you hadn't have saved her life. If there is anything else I can do to repay you, please let me know." Ben replied, handing him his business card.

"Not a problem. You take care now." The old man said with a wave and carried his dog under his arm.

Ben waved back and pulled away.

As he drove back to the house, he placed one hand on top of Abi's in hopes of getting a reaction.

Nothing.

She just continued to look straight ahead. Not even taking a second to blink.

They sat in silence all the way home, Ben worried terribly about her.

He pulled up outside his house and helped Abi from the car into the house.

He walked her upstairs to his bedroom and sat her on the bed.

Ben went to the airing cupboard and pulled out a warm blue towel and took her to the bathroom.

Still not a word as they walked across the landing.

In the bathroom, he turned the bath taps, poured some lavender bubble bath into the warm running water and lit some candles.

He undressed her slowly so as to not panic her in any way.

He helped her into the bath and as she sat amongst the fluffy, pearlescent bubbles, Ben plunged a sponge into the warm water, bringing it back out and pressed it onto her back gently.

"I'm sorry," Abi whispered finally.

"You have nothing to be sorry for Abi." He said calmly to her.

"Why were you down there?" He asked.

"I don't know. I don't remember even leaving your house. I was dreaming about Katrina down by the river and that's when that man found me. He must have thought I was crazy." Abi cried, hot tears stung her cheeks.

"No of course not! He was just worried about you." Ben assured her,

Ben continued to sponge her back, squeezing it so the water trickled down her back.

"Why would Katrina even lead me there?" She sobbed.

"I don't know. Maybe it wasn't even Katrina. We all know that Helen woman is a nasty piece of work. She tried to have me dead last night. As horrible as it sounds, maybe you were next on her list. I'll have to try and get a hold of Jack later and see how he and Luna are." Ben replied.

73

"I went to your house first this morning looking for you. Things were all over the place again in there, your dressing table mirror had been knocked over again, there were books on the floor and the mirror was faced down on the floor. I believe Katrina had sent me a message to come find you in the mirror and perhaps this Helen didn't want you to be found, perhaps it was face down on the floor in hopes that no-one would read it. I'm just glad that Katrina is on our side, or at least I believe her to be." Ben explained.

"Thank you for being with me through all of this. I really don't know what I'd do without you." Abi said, as she reached to hold Ben's hand, tears still in her bloodshot eyes.

Ben held her hand tightly and pulled her as close as he could without actually getting into the tub. His white t-shirt went see-through from the wetness of Abi's hair on his chest. He Kissed her forehead gently.
Abi turned slightly to face him and kissed his soft lips slowly.
He stood and pulled his wet t-shirt over his head revealing a toned stomach and muscular chest with lightly scattered dark hair.
He bent down and lifted Abi from the bath, water dripping all over his body from her naked, wet skin.

He carried her along the hallway, water dripping onto the soft, pile carpet as he headed towards the bedroom. He kicked the door open softly with his foot and laid her onto the bed.

Chapter 14

Ben got out of bed, body sweaty from pleasure, and headed to the bathroom for a quick shower to freshen up.

Abi laid in bed, heart still pounding and legs weak. She shut her eyes for just a second, but that's all it seemed to take now before she was back to having another dream.

Katrina sat in a hall with a soft, brown blanket draping over her knees. A look of fear in her eyes but not moving a muscle. She sat there, looking out of the window, missing her little Henry and wishing him to be back in her arms for a warm cuddle. Oh what she would do to have him back with her.

Today was visiting day but over the last two months, James' visits became so irregular that they were now non-existent. He used to come twice a week, every Wednesday and Sunday, well that was the first three weeks. From week four, the visits went down to just Sundays. She had not seen him now for two weeks.

Each week, every visit, Katrina would prove how she had improved by showing him nurse reports of her behaviour and not needing therapy as often and that she may even be able to have an early release. James didn't seem to show much interest in how well she was doing or the fact that she could be out earlier than expected.

Without the visits and support from her husband, Katrina looked like she had taken a turn for the worse. Her hair was all knotted, her skin pale, she looked as though she had given up on life.

She slowly started rocking backwards and forwards, her lips seemed to be mouthing words but not speaking them out loud. The rocking became more aggressive and she finally snapped.

"I want my baby! She's going to kill my baby! She may have fooled my idiot husband, but she will never fool me! She's the one that should be in here! Not me!" Katrina shouted, as she stood up from her hard, wooden chair, the blanket falling to the ground revealing a long white nightdress.

"Katrina, you need to calm down." a nurse advised.

"No, I will not calm down! How would you feel if your husband didn't believe you, that your baby was in trouble hey? How would you feel if everyone thought that you were crazy when in fact you were telling the truth?!" Katrina screamed back at her.

"I warned you Katrina." The nurse replied and ordered 2 security men to restrict her and take her down to the water therapy room.

"No, you shall not put me through that again! I am telling the truth I tell you, damn it!" Katrina shouts, kicking her legs and trying hard to release herself from the men's grips.

They held her tight by each arm, their fingers leaving bright, purple bruises on her delicate skin. They dragged her to the water therapy room where the head nurse was waiting. She instructs the men to unclothe her. With a great struggle, they managed to get her nightdress over her head revealing her pale, naked skin.

They tied her hands with some rope and a towel around her feet and placed her into the cold, metal tub.

The head nurse proceeded to turn on the cold water tap to fill the bath whilst Katrina laid in it.

The water was freezing, it was like ice on her already cold skin. Katrina lay there shaking and begging to be let out and that she promised that she would be better.

"You were warned Katrina. You know this sort of behaviour will not be tolerated. You're meant to be a young woman, not a wild animal. This treatment will help your mind be better." The nurse told her, as if completely confident that this treatment was the best thing for her.

And with that, the nurse pulled Katrina's feet upwards, plunging Katrina's head into the sharp, icy waters of the tub. Tens of thousands of bubbles gurgled to the surface

as Katrina screamed from under the water and tried to kick her legs frantically. Her body threw itself off of each side of the bath as she struggled to breathe.
Just as her screams started to silent, the nurse pushed Katrina's feet back into the water, pushing her head back up out of the scary, deathly waters.

But Katrina knew this method far too well. As much as she would love to believe this terrifying torture was over, she knew it was not.

After gasping as many breaths as she could, the nurse suddenly plunged Katrina's head back under the freezing, rippling waters.

This time Katrina held her breath for as long as she could. She looked up to the top of the water hoping angels would come and take her away. Pinks and blues swirl in front of her eyes in the water making soothing, pretty patterns until the world went dark before her.

Noticing that Katrina had finally passed out, the nurse once more pushed Katrina's feet into the water bringing her head back up. She ordered the 2 men to take her back to her room.

One of the men reached into the silver, metal tub and lifted Katrina's limp body from the glacial waters. The other man carried her nightdress and blanket.
They both walked out of the water therapy room and down the white, clinical hallway. They passed several doors and rooms on their way. Patients were standing in doorways and along the corridors giving the men disapproving, evil looks. One woman with short, scraggly hair mimicked a dog and did one loud bark at them as they passed, making them jump and sway to one side. The rest of the patients started laughing as they continued to walk down the corridor.

"Do you all want a turn in the treatment room?" The man holding Katrina turned and threatened them all. All the patients hurried into their rooms, scared of ANY type of treatment this place had to offer. There was silence for the rest of their walk to Katrina's room.

Katrina's room had white brick walls, a murky window that you could barely see out of covered by black, metal bars. One wooden desk and a rickety, paint-chipped chair.
Paper sat on the desk but no pens or pencils were to be seen. And finally 1 black, metal-framed bed, with a squeaky, spring mattress that was hard and lumpy. The most difficult thing to try and rest on, let alone get to sleep.

The man who was carrying Katrina laid her down on her solid, uncomfortable bed and left the room.

The other man seemed different. He shut the door to the room. The yellow light flickered above them both. He pulled Katrina forward and dressed her back in her nightgown. He laid her back down gently and placed her blanket over her. He checked her pulse to make sure it was steady. He picked up her hand delicately, leans down to her ear and whispered, "I'm so sorry. I will get you out of here." A tear fell from his closed eyes and onto her cold skin.

He got up and left her room, locking the door behind him.

Katrina woke up as if she had just had an electric shock pass right through her body. She then realised where she was, turned onto her side, hugged her knees and started to cry.

Abi stepped towards Katrina, fully aware that Katrina couldn't see or feel her, sat on the bed next to her and placed her hand on her shoulder in hopes that she may feel some comfort.

"Abi." A male voice called in the distance.
She stood and walked out of Katrina's room into the corridor.
"Abi wake up." She heard Ben's voice and her eyes opened wide.

"Abi, you've been out of it for hours! With everything going on I thought I'd let you sleep. It's seven o'clock and you've not eaten anything all day." Ben said to her, hand on her warm shoulder.
"Oh my god really?! You should have woken me up sooner. I'm sorry." Abi apologised with sleepy eyes.
"You need to stop apologising so much Abi, you're going through a lot. We both are, but you more so." Ben insisted, as he sat on the bed with a bowl of soup on a tray for her.
"Thank you," Abi replied, sitting up to finally eat something.

"I had another dream... or vision... whatever you want to call them. It wasn't nice at all." Abi told him and took a sip of her soup.
Ben climbed up next to her and put an arm around her to comfort her.
"Katrina was in the Asylum. They put her through the cold water treatment, the bath one where they drown the patient until they pass out. I watched them do it to her. Twice they did it." A tear fell down her cheek and into her soup.

78

"Oh Abi," Ben said in a comforting voice.

"There was nothing I could do. One of the security men seemed to want to help her though. Although he had to do what he was told by the head nurse and doctors, he felt sympathetic towards her and even whispered to her when she was unconscious saying that he's sorry and he will get her out."

"As in, break her out? Help her escape?" Ben asked curiously.

"I'm not sure. Either that or when it comes time for her to leave, he would take her away from the place. She went through so much torture there. She hadn't done anything wrong. She just wanted to be with her baby and for them both to be safe. And that good for nothing husband stopped visiting her after a couple of weeks, leaving her lonely and feeling worthless. Scumbag!" Abi said angrily.

"I've got an idea," Ben announced. "Does the asylum still exist?" Ben asked.

"I believe so," Abi replied. "I think it got shut down about 30 years ago and it was left abandoned from what I read."

"Do you know where it is located?"

"I think it's just off the A21, it's in the countryside near to Sevenoaks I believe," Abi advised.

"That's not far, about a 30 minutes drive!" Ben hinted.

"You want to go and check the place out don't you?" Abi asked.

"Don't you?" Ben asked back in reply.

"Only because you've mentioned it." She said with a smile.

"Why don't we see if Jack and Luna want to come along? I spoke to Jack earlier and Luna is very worn out after last night, being possessed and all, so she may want to stay home but I can check with them. I know Jack wouldn't want to miss out on a more than likely haunted location." Ben suggested.

"Yeah go for it!" Abi agreed.

"I'll give him a call," Ben said, leaning over and kissing her.

Ben got up from the bed and headed out to the hallway to call Jack.

Abi got up and went for a shower. Their rather heart racing activity from this morning and her terrifying dream had made her feel a bit sweaty. She needed to feel refreshed and made a note in her head to change the bedding once she was out of the bath.

Ben got a hold of Jack.

"Hey. How are you both feeling now?" Ben asked Jack.

"Yeah we're okay. We've both had a sleep and feel a bit more human now. Think we all needed a day to relax." Jack replied.

"Yeah, tell me about it. After this morning, Abi basically slept all day, although I'm not sure she actually rested. She had another dream about Katrina, when she was in the Asylum. She had to watch them put Katrina through the cold water treatment. It really upset her."

"Well that sucks! She can't seem to catch a break can she?!" Jack replied.

"Nope. So I was wondering... Abi and I are going to the Blue Waters Asylum to have a look around. It was abandoned 30 years ago." Ben informed him.

"Feel up to joining us? We understand if you don't want to or if Luna still needs to rest. She must be exhausted still from last night." Ben asked.

"Count me in! You know I can't resist a possibly haunted location. Luna needs more rest though, it really took it out of her last night." Jack replied..

"Yeah, that's understandable." Ben sympathised. "We want to go down during the day to find it and have a look about before it gets dark, possibly come up with a plan of which rooms we want to investigate for the night and all that."

"Sounds good to me! As it's just the 3 of us, we could all head down in the van. I could pick you both up at 11 am, grab some lunch when we get there, then head to the location?" Jack suggested.

"Perfect!" Ben agreed.

"See you tomorrow morning then!" Jack replied.

"See you tomorrow!" Ben said in return and hung up.

Abi came out of the bathroom wrapped in a towel, steam following her out of the door and water from her hair dripping down her back.

"Jack is 100% up for joining us tomorrow and has offered to pick us up in his van. Luna will be skipping this one. Last night got the better of her. It must have been terrifying to be taken over like that." Ben said.

"Fab!" Abi replied. "Not about Luna but that Jack is up for joining us, Just makes me feel a bit better having people with us that have experience in this type of thing," Abi explained.

"I know what you mean," Ben replied. "Jack will be here at 11 am tomorrow and we will be getting lunch on the way to the Asylum." Ben continued. "It feels so weird to say that. We're going to the Asylum!" Ben laughed.

"I wouldn't be laughing just yet!" Abi replied and went in for a hug. "Come on you. We need to change those sheets and get some rest." Abi said, taking his hand and pulled him towards the bedroom.

Chapter 15

Ben woke up to a sunny Wednesday morning. Just a slither of sunlight coming from behind the curtain, the sound of birds singing from the stone birdbath in the garden.

He headed downstairs, popped on his black, striped apron that had seen better days and started rummaging about in the cupboards. He brought out a bag of croissants, headed across the kitchen to the American style fridge, opened the door and took out some eggs and a pack of unsmoked bacon.

Meanwhile, Abi awoke to the smell of bacon cooking, wafting up the stairs. She climbed out of bed and drew the curtains. The cool bedroom filled with warm sunlight. She put her fluffy, white dressing gown on and made her way downstairs.

"Oh hello naked chef!" Abi laughed, as Ben handed her a plate with freshly cooked croissants, eggs and bacon, cheekily showing his naked bottom.
Ben kissed her on the cheek as she took the plate and took her seat at the dining table.
Ben collected his plate and joined Abi at the table and they enjoyed their breakfast together, finally experiencing some normality.

"It was nice to lay in for once and not have any dreams. It's like I was given a break!" Abi joked.
"It was good to wake up and see you sleeping so peacefully." Ben smiled.

"So do you reckon we will get anything tonight?" Ben asked, as he cut into his runny egg.

"It's an Asylum Ben! If we don't get any of our spirits through, I'm pretty sure others will be there. Will be good for Jack either way." Abi replied with a mouth full of food.

"Yeah that's true," Ben agreed, as he finished his last mouthful.

"That was yummy Ben, thank you. The croissants were so buttery!" Abi thanked him, overly satisfied with her breakfast.

Ben looked up at the large, station house style clock on the wall.

"One hour until Jack gets here. We should start getting ready." Ben said, as he collected the plates and took them through to the kitchen.

Abi tucked her chair in and walked back up the stairs to get washed and dressed.

She put on a pair of black jeans and a white, ribbed tank top. Then hunted around the bedroom in search of maybe a gym bag or overnight bag that they could store some extra clothes in for the night investigation.

Bingo.

One large gym bag in the bottom of Ben's messy closet, which surprised her as the rest of the house is spotless.

She opened it up and found a spare pair of white socks with red trim and a rusty padlock.

She removed the padlock and left the socks in the bag. Then grabbed another pair of jeans and a black hoodie from his chest of drawers and placed them in the bag.

Now she just needed some spare clothes for herself... which of course were back at her house.

"I really need to bring more of my clothes over here until things settle down," Abi whispered to herself.

Ben walked into the bedroom, now completely naked and which didn't seem to bother him one bit. And why should it with a body like that?!

Abi smiled as a pink shade floods her face.

"All the washing up is done, I just need to get dressed," Ben said, heading to his closet.

"I've packed some extra clothes for you for tonight. We don't know what the conditions will be like so I thought, ``better safe than sorry." Abi explained, not knowing where to look.

"Good idea. Thank you." Ben replied as he pulled on his dark blue jeans and did up the zip and fastened his button.

"I just need to head over to mine and grab more clothes as well. I was thinking I'd grab some to keep here too if that's okay? Just until things settle down. I'm not moving in." She smiled.
"Yeah that's fine, we can head over now." He replied, pulling his white t-shirt over his head.

They both descended downstairs.
Ben grabbed his keys from the side, flung the gym bag over his back and headed to her house.

He unlocked her front door and checked around before entering. He gave the all-clear and they headed upstairs to Abi's room.
Surprisingly, the house was silent. Nothing was out of place. Everything felt normal for once.
Abi headed over to her white, French-style wardrobe. She took out a spare top, baggy, black hoodie and another pair of jeans. Looking down at her dolly shoes she decided to grab a pair of ankle boots for later.

Drip.

Abi felt a drop of water hit her head. She looked up and saw a puddle of water collecting on the ceiling.
"Oh crap!" Abi said thinking there was a burst pipe.
They headed up the tower to the library that sat above Abi's bedroom.
They lifted the newly fitted carpet that was situated above her room.
Ben looked around the room for a tool to lift the floorboard. Seeing a screwdriver on the shelf, he strode over to it and returned to where Abi was standing, dropped to the floor and levered the floorboard up to reveal the pipes.
Looking in, there was no sign of water.
"Hahahahaha." A hushed laugh came from behind them.
Dropping what they were doing and grabbing their bags, they ran.
"Not today Helen!" Abi shouted, as they legged it down the stairs and out slamming the front door behind them.

At that very moment, Jack's van pulled up outside Ben's a little further down the street.

"Great timing!" Ben exclaimed. He took both bags and chucked them in the back of the van as Abi slid into the middle seat.

"So, what's new?" Jack asked with a smile. Just by looking at them both, he could tell something else had just happened and he wasn't surprised by anything at this point.
"Oh you know, water dripping from the ceiling, ghostly laughter, you know... the usual." Abi replied very casually, as if it was completely normal for these things to be happening. But of course, this did seem to be becoming the norm for them. Not a day went by without something creepy happening.

Ben slammed the back door making the whole van shake and jumped into the passenger seat next to Abi, in the front of the van.

"To the nuthouse!" Ben exclaimed, after plugging in his belt and rubbing his hands together.

Jack pulled out onto the main road, radio blaring Fall Out Boys 'Sugar we're going down'. They headed around a sharp corner and onto a long stretch of road out of town, down into a dip.
The road seemed to go on for miles. Tall, green, leafy trees lined the edge of the narrowing road.

After a couple of hours driving in the beautiful countryside, passing through rolling green fields and farmlands, the road widened as they approached a village.

It was a small village dotted with pretty, country cottages with thatched roofs and Tudor style buildings. On the left, a charming but dated pub with white walls, aged, black beams and wooden tubs filled with pink pansies and trailing ivy at the entrance.

"Who's hungry?" Jack asked, pointing out the approaching pub.
"Yes!" Both Ben and Abi said in unison excitedly, Abi's stomach was growling with hunger.

Jack pulled into a small car park to the side of the pub, which then revealed a big, beautiful garden with picnic benches, umbrellas, flowers and a small bbq area towards the back.

They all jumped out of the van and headed to a sunny picnic table in the middle of the garden and read the lunch menu.

Only a short menu but all the usual British classics.
Scampi and chips.

Fish and chips.
Burger and chips.
Ploughman's cheese board.
And finally a selection of paninis.

Ben chose a bacon and brie panini, Abi opted for the scampi and chips and Jack went for the Burger and chips. Jack wrote down the order and headed to the bar with their options, leaving Abi and Ben at the table soaking up the sun.

"It's good to be outside enjoying the sunshine for a bit." Ben sighed, his eyes closed facing the sun.
"Yeah I know, I'm quite glad it's not too hot though, I would have been sweating in these jeans," Abi replied.
"Yeah that's true, although, I don't mind you getting a bit sweaty," Ben said with a wink and reached out for Abi's hand.
"Oh shush." Abi laughed, as Jack walked back with their drinks on a tray.
"So, any nerves about tonight?" Jack asked as he placed the glasses of coke down on the worn, rickety table.

"Erm, I'm not really sure to be honest. A bit excited, a bit nervous. I'm eager to find out more information and hopefully get to the bottom of whatever is happening but, with everything that's been going on, I am a bit worried about anything negative that could happen. It's an asylum, there's bound to be lots of troubled souls still left behind." Abi said, reaching for her drink.
"I know what you mean. I've not done an investigation at an asylum before so this will be new territory for all of us." Jack confided to them both.

A lady wearing a black pencil skirt and white, crisp shirt arrived with their orders.
The waitress placed the plates on the table in front of them and asked if they needed anything else.

"Actually while you're here, do you know of the Blue Waters Asylum on the outskirts of the village?" Jack asked, pinching a chip from his plate with his fingers.
"Yes I do, very strange things happen there." She replied.
"Happen? As in, happening still?" Jack responded.
"Yep, police are up there at least once a month because of reports of noises and sightings. Last month a kid went up there at night with some friends and got caught playing with a Ouija board. There's not really a lot of things for kids to do around here you see. So sometimes they head to the asylum and mess about with things they shouldn't. A few years ago a girl even died there. It's said that she killed herself

in a bath there. No one in the village believes that, but what can you do if the police won't take it any further?"

"Oh that poor girl!" Abi said, with sorrow in her voice.

"Her name was Trina Adams, looks a bit like you actually which is weird." the waitress informed them looking at Abi and started to nervously play with her fingers. "She was a troubled girl, she went up to the Asylum a lot with friends but the last time she went, she was alone. So no one can explain what happened, but we know she wouldn't kill herself. Especially in a bath. She was scared of water and besides, there's no water running at the property, so the only way to fill a bath is to take your own water and she wouldn't have been able to get the amount needed there without being seen by someone." she explained.

"So are you planning on going up there then?" she questioned.
"Yes," Jack replied. "I'm a professional paranormal investigator. You may have seen some of my videos on Youtube. I receive calls to investigate lots of different properties all over the country. I usually have my sensitive medium friend with me but she has been through a lot recently so she's taking some time out."
"Oh yes, I know the ones! I thought I recognised you! Well feel free to add anything I've told you today into your next episode!" she replied excitedly.
"Your meal is on me!" She winked at Jack and turned to head back inside the pub.

"What can I say? The ladies love me!" Jack smiled all smug.
"Yeah, shame she didn't pay for all the meals," Ben said, a little jealous.

They finished off their meals and Jack left a £20 tip on the table, with a note for the waitress.

Thanks for the lovely service.
Wonderful, helpful waitress and welcoming pub. Will be back again.

They walked back to the van, belly's now full, to continue their trip to the Asylum just a 15-minute drive down the road.

They head down the street and away from the quaint country village, back onto straight roads through the countryside. At this point, the road didn't even seem like a road they should be on at all. A dirt track that was soon surrounded by water for about a mile until it turned into twisty, winding back country roads with blind bends, surrounded by ancient woodlands.

As they travelled deeper into the wooded area, the weather started to turn. Dark grey clouds loomed above them carrying a promise of electric storms. The van bumped up and down, trying to dodge the potholes in the now very stony road.
One large thud as they went over a small rock in the road and the radio cut out and went to white noise.

The trees along the edge of the road started to thin and it became clear that these trees didn't have leaves, and the ground was just dry dirt covered with nettles and twigs that may have once resembled bushes. Everything except the weeds were dead. No sign of any wildlife to be seen, not even a bird.

The sky blackened so much you would confuse it for a night sky. The clouds started to rumble loudly as the rain seemed to suddenly pour like a tap that had just been turned on full blast, making it difficult to see. A bolt of lightning struck the road right in front of them and seemed to outline a shadow of a woman.
Jack swerved as quickly as he could to avoid the deadly bolt and the figure they had just seen right in front of their eyes. Brakes screeching and wheels sliding on the soaked, muddy road, the car hurtled off the road and into a ditch in the dark, black woodlands.

After a couple of seconds of silence, Abi sounded off with a moan.
"Is everyone okay?" she asked, as she realised the van was on its side and the only thing holding her in place was her seat belt.
"Yeah I'm okay," Ben replied.
"I hit my head," Jack said, turning his head towards them, revealing blood dripping from a cut.
"Jack you're bleeding!" Abi exclaimed.
"Right we need to get out of here so we can sort that out," Ben said looking around the van.
"The only option we've got is to kick the windscreen out Jack," Ben confirmed as he looked at the cracked window.
"Yeah let's just do it," Jack replied.
"Okay, on three we all kick the windscreen okay?" Ben instructed. "One.. two.. THREE!"

SMASH!

Rather than the whole windscreen falling out, it shattered into pieces sending shards of wet glass all over the boggy ground.

"Jack, you'll need to get out first as you're closest to the ground. Then you Abi, but be careful of the glass." Ben explained to them in a leader-like fashion.

Jack unbuckled his belt and fell against the door. He stumbled as he climbed over the steering wheel and airbag that was smoking from underneath. He pulled himself through the windscreen and fell into a muddy puddle soaking his knees as he knelt in the mud.

"Your turn Abi," Jack called to her in the pouring rain as more thunder rumbled high above them.

Abi tried to turn her body whilst still in her seat so that her feet were facing the ground to her right. Once in position, she undone her belt and landed with her feet on the window making it crack underneath her. Jack held out his hand for Abi to hold onto as she pulled herself through.

Ben followed Abi's plan and positioned himself accordingly so that he would also land on his feet. He climbed out of the windscreen and joined Abi and Jack in the pouring rain.

They grabbed their bags from the back of the van and any equipment they're able to carry between them. They were able to squeeze some camera equipment into Ben's gym bag and the rest were all in large plastic carry cases.

Abi checked her phone and noticed that she had no signal to call for help. Jack and Ben checked theirs too, waving them at arm's length above their heads. Nothing!

Ben cleaned up Jack's cut, placed a plaster on it, not too sure whether it would stay on in this rain. After a chat, they decided to head towards the Asylum as it was possibly closer than the village

The storm above became louder and the ground seemed to vibrate in response to the ever-growing loud rumbles in the sky. White flashes lit up the darkness surrounding them and they saw a dark, looming building in the distance ahead of them. Their feet were now soaked and squelching from the waterlogged road, clothes drenched through as if they had been sitting in water for days on end. They were quite essentially drowned rats at this time. Luckily their bags were waterproof so their spare clothes, which Abi had ingeniously thought to pack this morning, would be nice and dry when they finally reached their destination.

Chapter 16

An old, white, wooden sign that had seen better days, was swinging on its last rusty hinge as they approached the large, iron gates to the Asylum.
They could just make out the name of the Asylum on the sign, made difficult to read by the crusty, peeling paint and the current storm.

The gate to the property was at least twice their size and although rusty as hell, it was still standing strong. A silver, chunky padlock and chain were wrapped around the middle bars of the gate, holding it closed so that no one could trespass. It looked fairly new. Probably put in place to keep the local teenagers out after all of their previous shenanigans.
There was no way to climb over the gate and the fence surrounding the building was just as high as the gate itself. The only thing they could do was split up and try to find a gap in the fence somewhere.

"Abi, you and Jack go that way, I'll go this way and we can meet in the middle," Ben instructed, pointing to the right of the fence as he started to walk in the opposite direction.
"You can't go on your own!" Abi demanded, fearing his safety.
"Look, we can find a way in quicker if we split up, I'm not letting you go on your own and I know Jack will keep you safe," Ben explained. He unzipped his bag, pulled out 2 walkie talkies and handed one to Abi. "If anything happens, you can reach me on this, but I'm sure everything will be fine." He reassured her.
"Come on Abi." Jack encouraged as he put a hand on her soaked shoulder.

"Be careful," Abi said. She kissed him on the lips and squeezed him as hard as she could before pulling away and walking in the opposite direction with Jack.

Turning his back to the pair walking away, Ben took his torch from his bag. So far, they had been sharing one torch between them, to save battery life. He pushed the rubber button on the side and the light bulb flickered. He whacked it hard against his hands a couple of times and the light streamed ahead of his muddy path. He clipped the walkie talkie to his jacket and followed the fence.

The ground was littered with beer bottles, empty crisp packets and fag ends. Evidence that kids still came up here and because they couldn't get in, they just hung around on the borders getting wasted.

Hearing a twig snap on the floor behind him, he twisted around shining his torch in the direction of the noise in the woods to his left.
Two eyes were glowing from behind the trees. He started to walk over slowly, squinting through the dark to try and see better.
"It's just a bloody deer!" He whispered annoyingly to himself with a big sigh, as the deer ran off into the depths of the trees.

Meanwhile, Jack and Abi were headed in the opposite direction.

"I wish we didn't have to split up like this." Abi said to Jack as she moved her torch from left to right.
The light from her torch reflected on a flat surface ahead. As they got closer, a large lake revealed itself and the fence went straight through it, with no way to get around.
Jack picked up a rock from the ground and threw it into the lake.
"Crap. Looks deep." Jack huffed, racking his brain as to how to get across.
"We're going to have to scale the fence to get to the other side." He continued.
"Great," Abi replied in frustration.
"No way are my boots going to fit in those gaps. I've got to put my dolly shoes on and have TWO pairs of wet shoes."
"Sorry Abi, I can't see any other way to get over it."
"I know. Sorry, it's not your fault, it's just frustrating." She apologised as she removed the bag from her back.

Abi takes out her dolly shoes and replaces them with her fleece-lined boots, her feet now cold and wet.
"Whose great idea was this?" She asked sarcastically.

Jack laughed as Abi chucked her bag back on her back.

"I'll go first to check if it's safe." He insisted, making sure his bag was tight and secure on his shoulders. The last thing he wanted was for the bag to fall into the lake and lose thousands of pounds worth of equipment.

After checking the zips were all done up and tightened his straps on his shoulders, he started to climb the fence, squeezing his feet between the bars of the iron fencing, leaving orange, rusty marks on his black trainers after each step.

After gaining some height, he started to strafe right, making his way across the murky lake.

He gave Abi the go-ahead to start following in his footsteps.

She slid her dainty, saturated feet between the bars and started to climb her way towards Jack.

"Take it slowly." He called across to her.

"Well, there's no way I'm going fast. I can feel everything through the bottoms of these shoes, it's like I'm climbing barefooted and it hurts." Abi replied, wincing with each step she took.

Taking their time as they continued across, Abi took a second to look over the lake with her torch.

As she brought the torch back towards where Jack was, she glimpsed something in the water. She put the light back in that direction and there floating on top of the water, she saw a body. Limbs spread out like a starfish, face down and with no sign of movement.

"Jack, Jack, JACK!" She cried out quickly, turning back to him and steadying herself so she didn't fall in from her hands shaking so violently.

"There's a body in the water! There's a bloody dead person in the lake!" She called out, terrified.

Jack pulled out his torch and scanned the lake for what Abi was talking about.

He panned his torch across the lake slowly but didn't find anything there. A few branches and lily pad, but certainly no bodies.

"Abi I can't see anything, are you sure it wasn't a trick of the light," he questioned.

"Of course I'm sure, look." She insisted, pointing her torch back in the same direction that she had just seen the body floating. To her amazement, it wasn't there.

"But it was just there Jack, I promise. I am not seeing things I swear." Abi implored, feeling confused.

"Well, whatever it was has gone now. I'm not saying you didn't see it, you could have, but there's nothing we can do now if it's vanished." He sympathised.
"What if it's a ghost? What about the spirit box?!" She asked.
"I mean, we can try. I can't get to it though so you'll have to make it over to me, open my bag and get it out but PLEASE be careful. This stuff is expensive." He informed her.
"Oh, not be careful as I might fall in then, thanks." She snorted, as she started to make her way over to him.
"Don't be funny, you know what I mean." He replied.

Abi came side by side with Jack, reached into his backpack and pulled out the spirit box. She pulled the zips back together and just to scare him, she pretended to drop the spirit box into the deep waters.

"Woah!" She cried out.
There's a splash in the water below them.
"Abi, please tell me you didn't just drop it." He said with his eyes closed and head against the cold, wet bars.
"I am so sorry Jack, how much was it?" She asked.
"You have got to be bloody kidding me!" The anger started to show in his voice.
"Yep."
"What do you mean.. yep?" He asked.
"Yep... I was kidding you." She said with a cheeky grin across her face and spirit box in her hand in front of his face.
"Abi.."
"Yeah?"
"If we make it across here and the spirits inside that nuthouse don't kill you... I WILL!" He said, a mix of relief and frustration in his voice.
"Sorry I couldn't help it." She giggled.

Jack took the spirit box from her and switched it on. White noise and radio shifting sounds came from within the box.

"Is anyone out there?" He called out.
Nothing to be heard apart from the shifting noises of the radio stations.
"Does anyone want to talk?" He called out again.
Out of nowhere, an almighty, high pitched banshee scream came from the box, making them both jump and Jack almost dropped the box into the water FOR REAL, but quickly caught it before it was lost forever.

He chucked the spirit box, still scanning channels, into his hoodie front pocket and they both made their way across the fence as quickly as they could.

"Ahhh!" Abi screamed out, as she sliced the side of her foot on the rusty metal.
"Abi! Are you okay?" Jack shouted across to her as they near the edge of the lake.
"Yes, just sliced my foot, keep going!" She shouted, just wanting to get back onto land and bandage her foot up.

Jack reached the edge and jumped down from the fencing and waited for Abi to join him.
"Only a few more steps Abi!" He called out to her.
"Yeah, easy for you to say." She said sarcastically, as blood trickled from her foot and dripped into the waters below.
She held onto the fence with both hands, her good foot between the bars and her bloody foot behind her in the air. She hopped carefully as she gripped the bars and finally reached the end.

Jack held out his hands to her to help her jump down. As she landed, her ankle gave way and she fell to the waterlogged ground.
Jack flung his bag from his back and retrieved the first aid kit from the bottom.
He cleaned up the cut on Abi's foot with an alcohol wipe, put some cotton wool over the cut and wrapped it in a bandage. He carefully put her boot back on her foot to stop the dressing from getting wet. He then pulled out an ankle support for her other foot which had given way beneath her as she landed. Once her ankle was secure, Abi put her other boot on and wiggled her feet about to make sure she had full movement in them still.

All foot movement signs were good, Abi stood up from the sodden ground beneath her, a bottom shaped puddle appeared instantly where she was just sitting.
She brushed her hands off and Jack put the kit back away in his bag.
"If we carry on like this, we're going to run out of supplies before we've even made it inside." He chuckled.

A thick bolt of lightning hit the lake behind them, scaring them out of their skin.
"Well that was lucky! We could have been fried on that fence!" Abi exclaimed.
In disbelief and shock, they turned and continued to follow the fence, hoping to be meeting with Ben soon.

On the other side of the asylum fence, Ben was walking through a wooded area. Still following the fence, when he tripped over what he believed was a tree root sticking out from the ground that he failed to see.

Laying on the ground, he got onto his knees and looked towards his feet.

That was no root he tripped on, but a handle. A big, round, dirty, metal handle. He knelt beside it and brushed off all the mud, twigs and litter from the area to reveal a metal trap door.

He twisted and pulled the handle in all different ways, but it was no use. It didn't want to budge. He would have to speak to Jack and Abi about this. Maybe Jack has something they could use to get it open.

He stood, brushed off his knees and continued to follow the fence around. He walked and walked but there were no signs of anywhere to get through, over or under the fence. He took a seat on a nearby log that had fallen to think.

Sitting there, rain still managing to hit him through the branches of the trees, he wondered if they would find a way in. He twisted his wrist to look at his watch. 4 pm. They should have been inside already and have everything set up. They would have had a look about and made a plan of action.

That will not be happening. If they ever gain entry, they would just have to go with the flow, completely blind to what rooms there are and have no idea where they would be heading.

He was starting to feel defeated.

Snap.

He heard more twigs break up ahead of him.

He jumped down behind the large, dark log he had just been sitting on. He peeped over the log and saw two bright lights headed his way.

He grabbed his walkie talkie and pushed the button on the side.

"Abi, Jack. Stop walking." He demanded, releasing the button.

"Why?" Abi's voice came through.

"Just do it, now."

The lights stopped moving and stayed completely still.

"Thank god it's you two." He spoke into the walkie talkie. "I just had to check, I'm straight ahead of you." He said, coming out from behind the log.

"Were you hiding?" Jack asked with a laugh as they finally met back up with Ben.

"Well I didn't know whether you were police checking the perimeter or something, did I?" Ben said defensively.

"Did you find a way in?"

"No, you?" Abi asked.

"No. I did find a door hatch though, but I couldn't get it open. I thought maybe that could be a way in, but I couldn't lift it."

"Where abouts was it? I have a crowbar in my bag." Jack said.

"What else do you have in that Mary Poppins bag of yours?" Abi laughed.

"That would be telling wouldn't it." He smiled.

"Anyway, it's just down here," Ben tells them and lead the way back to the hidden door in the ground.

They reached the trap door. Jack gave it a quick tug.

"Okay, yeah I see what you mean." He said.

"Did you really think I was just being weak?" Ben asked with a frown.

"No, no. Just wanted to see how stuck it was." Jack replied, as he pulled out the crowbar from his backpack.

He managed to just about fit it in the lip of the door and started pushing the other end, like a lever, down to the ground... or at least trying to push it down.

"Ben, Abi. Pull the handle would you while I push on this end."

Abi and Ben both took the handle and started to pull.

Jack once again started pushing down on the crowbar and he could feel a little movement.

"Keep pulling." He said through gritted teeth.

And as soon as he said it, the door flew open, sending Ben and Abi shooting through the air and landing in a puddle of mud. No water. Just wet, runny mud.

"Great!" Abi said sarcastically.

Jack peered down the square hole in the ground, while Abi and Ben sorted themselves out.

It was so dark down there, that he couldn't see a thing. It smelt damp, old and musky. He grabbed his torch from his pocket and shone it down.

It was so deep he couldn't see the bottom. There was a ladder though.

"You two stay here for a sec, I'm going to head down, see how far it is and make sure it's safe," Jack said, putting his bag back on his back and tightened the straps once again.

"Be careful," Abi replied as Ben helped her back up.

"Pass me the walkie talkie Abi, that way I can let you know when to come down."

She un-clipped it from her top and handed it to him.

"See you in a bit." He said as he started to descend the ladder into darkness.

Jack held the end of the torch in his mouth as he used both hands to carefully travel down the ladder. Looking at the walls around him, he noticed scratch-like markings in the brick, as if someone had really dug their nails into the walls and dragged them down the stone.

Jack gulped heavily, a knot starting to form in his stomach as he went further down.

The walls were wet, the ladder was wet. He was so fed up with himself and everything he touched being wet.

He looks back up to the top of the ladder where he came in, the hole now looking more like a pinprick. He must be nearing the bottom now.

But instead of reaching the bottom, he stumbled upon a tunnel leading off part way down.

He held down the button on the walkie talkie, still attached to his jacket.

"Hey guys, I've not reached the bottom yet but there is a tunnel part way down. I think I'm near the bottom but might be worth checking out this other tunnel too." He suggested.

"Yeah sure. Get to the bottom first though. We will start making our way down to join you." Ben replied.

"Sure thing," Jack confirmed back and continued down to the bottom.

Ben started to head down the ladder, followed by Abi.

"Nice view," Ben smirked as he looked up, Abi above him, tight jeans clinging to her curves.

"Eye's down please!" She tried to sound serious, but she couldn't help but smile in the dank darkness.

After 5 minutes of descending downwards, they came across the same tunnel Jack had mentioned moments before.

Ben flashed his torch down the tunnel but the light just reflected from wall to wall due to the amount of water collecting on the surfaces.

"Hang on," Ben said. He leant over and climbed onto the tunnel ledge.

"I'm coming with you." She demanded and followed him into the tunnel.

They had to crouch over slightly as the ceiling was a bit lower than expected, but not low enough that they had to crawl, which they were happy about.

The tunnel wasn't very long but as they neared the end, they came across another gate. Through the gate, on the other side, there seemed to be another drop. This gate however hadn't stood the test of time. The hinges were broken.

Ben lifted the gate and moved it to one side, so they could approach the edge and see down.

Looking down, they realised they were standing midway down what seemed to be a well. The walls were coated in green, wet fungi. Ben panned his torch around looking to see if there were any other tunnels leading off from the well. He couldn't find any, but what they did find, they didn't like.

Over towards the back of the well was a small ledge. Laying on the ledge, a human skeleton, one arm hanging off the edge, in the water.

They both gasped and ran back towards the ladder and went down as fast as they could.

They continued down to join Jack at the bottom of the tunnels.

The sounds of water dripping echoed all around them.

They finally reached the ground where Jack was waiting for them.

"What took you guys so long?" Jack asked, trying to be funny.

"While I was waiting for you both, I walked ahead to have a look about. No other tunnels lead off from here but at the end of this path is another ladder going back up to, I'm guessing, the surface. Who knows, maybe even the Asylum." He informed them.

"Okay, but first... we went down the tunnel," Ben admitted to him.

"You went without me?!" Jack replied feeling a little left out. "Well, what was down there then?" He asked.

"Not anything nice, that's for sure," Abi affirmed.

"It leads to a well. But it was what was within the well that was creepy. There was a skeleton laying on the edge with his hand just dangling in the water!" Ben explained.

"You're kidding!" Jack gasped in disbelief.

"Do our faces look like we're kidding?" Abi asked, her skin pale and a frightened expression in her eyes.

"I guess not," Jack replied apologetically.

"Anyway, let's check out where this tunnel leads then. It's about time we get into that bloody building." Ben said in frustration as another hour passed.

They all head down the dark, dripping tunnel. Slime all over the walls and long, furry looking algae hanging from the ceiling.

They reached the end of the tunnel and started to head up the ladder. This one was thankfully a lot shorter than the first. Jack got to the top and pushed the hatch upwards.

It opened straight away.

He climbed a few more steps and looked around.

"Guys... we're in!"

Chapter 17

The trio climbed out from the tunnels, so grateful to finally be somewhere dry.
Abi pulled the bag off of her back and started dragging dry clothes out straight away.
"I am not staying in these disgusting, wet clothes a moment longer. Can you turn around please so I can change?" Abi asked.
Jack turned around and faced the opposite direction, while Ben continued to look at Abi.
"You too please!" She said to Ben,smiling.
"I've already seen you naked though."
"Have you now?!" Jack asked with an excited smile.
Ben threw him an 'I'll tell you all about it later' kind of smile as he turned and looked away from Abi.
"Thanks Ben." She said, as he continued to smile to himself.

Ben and Jack took a look at the room around them.
They were standing in what seemed to be the head doctor's office.
A desk towards the back of the room, upon it, a long, wooden block engraved with a name.

Dr Arthur Watson.
Head of Blue Waters Hospital.

"Watson... Why does that name ring a bell?" Ben questioned quietly to himself.

Books and papers were all over the floor. Cabinet drawers open, with paper hanging out of them, presumably old patient records.

Smashes in the windows and what looked to be devil worship type graffiti on the walls. The door to the office lay on the floor as if someone had previously kicked it open, sending it flying off of its hinges and leaving it where it landed.
The place was a mess.

Abi jumped up as she pulled up her dry jeans and did up the button.
"There. That's so much better." She said, finally feeling a little more comfortable.
She finally looked around and took in the room.
"Wow. What a crap hole this is." She stated bluntly.
"Yep. Seems kids have really gone to town here." Jack replied.

Abi headed through the doorway, stepping over the beaten up, old door.
She now stood in what looked to be the nurse's reception area and lobby.
"This must be the entrance and waiting room." Abi guessed pointing over to the large oak doors on the other side of the room. She walked across the lobby, a gigantic glass chandelier sat shattered in the middle of the room. Shards of glass, pottery and books all over the floors. She reached the door and turned the brass knob. The door opened with a loud slow squeak and scratching noise as it opened against the rubbish on the floor.
Once open, they could see outside. The drive, the old, marble fountain in the centre and finally, the large iron gate and fence surrounding and protecting the property.

"This place would have looked so stunning back then," Abi said admirably. She had always loved architecture, especially that of the Victorian era.
"Yeah, I bet the patients thought so too until they got inside," Jack replied sarcastically.
"You know what I mean. If you forget about the fact it's an asylum and maybe think of it as, I don't know, a spa retreat. It would be beautiful."
"Yeah... I'm sorry I just can't picture it. Knowing what happened here and looking at how degraded it is.. in my mind, it's just another horrible haunted building." Jack replied.
"You don't know that it's haunted yet," Ben said to him.

BANG

The sound of a door slamming shut from upstairs echoed through the building.
"You were saying..." Jack replied smugly, starting to prep his equipment.
Abi and Ben both start to do the same and empty their bags of any equipment they managed to squeeze in. Ben handed Jack the plastic cases with the camera equipment inside.

He set up one camera in the corner of the lobby area, making sure to get the reception area in focus too. Another in the doctor's office, capturing the entirety of the room and doorway.

They then headed up the stairs to the 1st-floor landing overlooking the lobby area, above the reception desk.

The stairway was grand. A thick dark oak bannister, with a straggly, stained, faded carpet going up the many steps. From the looks of it, it used to be red, but you couldn't be one hundred percent sure due to how dirty it was. The staircase had a beautiful curved design as it led you to the landing.

At the top of the stairs to the left, there seemed to have been a doorway at one point, however, it had since been bricked up. From the outside to the left would have been the left wing. This would have been where they had all the therapy rooms.

As they couldn't get into the left wing, they headed right, along the balcony and down the hall. At the end of the balcony where it turns into the hallway, the carpet ended and wooden floorboards, with bits of broken, scattered tiles continued down the rest of the hall. The walls were white, wooden panels. Again covered in graffiti and by the looks of it, black mould.

"Here, we're going to need these," Jack said, holding out white dust masks. "There's black mould all over these walls. The fumes it gives off are not safe to inhale." He informed them both.

They took the masks and fit the elastic straps over their ears, masks covering their nose and mouth.

There were doors on both sides of the hallway. Quite surprisingly, still attached to their frames! Some wide open, some shut.

Jack set up a camera at the top of the stairs facing down the hall where Ben and Abi were walking. They reached the first room on the left. The door was already open. Ben took the handheld camera from his bag and switched it on. The small recording light on top of the camera turned red to show it was recording. He stepped inside the room.

It was a small box room. The walls had crumbled away. On one wall, someone seemed to have punched a hole. Looking through this hole you could see the room next door.

A brass and iron bedstead was pushed up against one wall. On top of the rusty, old frame was a filthy mattress that seemed to have been ripped apart, springs poking through the grubby material. Surprisingly, the window was still intact and not shattered to pieces by little thugs throwing rocks through it.

Looking through the murky window, you could just about see the bars covering the glass on the other side. Presumably there to stop the patients from committing suicide.

"Where do you think that door slamming came from?" Abi asked.

"Well it sounded close by when we were downstairs, so it must have been one of the rooms closest to the balcony. Maybe the room opposite." Ben suggested.

They headed out of the room, Ben still acting as the cameraman.

Abi led the way and Ben focused the camera on her. She crossed the hall and approached the closed door opposite. She took the EMF detector from inside her jacket pocket. She switched it on and slowly waved it around the door to see if there was any energy surrounding the door.

As her hand moved to the handle of the door, the needle on the device shot to the middle of the gauge to show an energy was there.

She moved it away from the handle.. nothing. Back to the handle and it spiked again.

"Hey guys! It just spiked! There's something here." She exclaimed as she got Ben to film the activity.

"Got it!" Ben said in excitement.

Abi slowly put her hand on the cold handle and pushed it down.

It creaked as she slowly opened the door, her torchlight revealed a Ouija board painted onto the wooden floorboards of the messy, vandalised room.

"Well someone's been busy in here." She whispered, as she nodded in the direction of the painted circle of letters on the floor.

"Awesome!" Jack said excitedly as he rushed past Ben. "We could use this later to gain communication."

"Is that really safe?" Abi asked, sounding concerned. She had never used a spirit board before, but she had heard many stories and they didn't always end well. People going insane thinking the Devil was after them, spirits following them home and even being killed!

"It is if you know what you're doing!" Jack confirmed.

"It's only those that have no experience and don't protect themselves. They mess about and they don't know what or who they're messing about with." He continued.

They heard a squeak come from the hallway behind them. Like someone had just
stepped across a creaky floorboard.
Ben quickly panned his camera around as he stood in the doorway. He watched the
hallway on his night vision camera screen.
Nothing showed up.
"I can't see anything." He let Abi and Jack know. They were still standing in the Ouija
board room.

Something hit Abi's foot out of nowhere.
She looked down. Her foot was standing on the Hello that had been painted on the
floor and right next to her foot was a small red ball.
"Uh... guys... I'm standing on the Ouija board and a ball just hit my foot! I have no
idea where it came from." She said as she lifted her torch from her foot to the
opposite direction. Every hair on her body stood on end as a sense of panic started
to rise inside of her.

A table is sat at the other end of the room in darkness. Abi slowly walked towards
the table and noticed a shadow. She started to bend down as she walked ever
closer.
Closer and closer she went.
The bulb in her torch exploded and she screamed.
They all stood frozen to the spot.
Abi, still looking in the direction of the table, saw two red eyes start to open and
look straight at her.
She couldn't move. She was like a statue, frozen in time.
The shadow grew bigger and bigger, coming out from under the table and growing
until it hit the ceiling and rushed towards Abi screaming and ran straight through her
knocking her to the floor.

"Abi! Abi!" Both Ben and Jack called her name, removed her mask and shook her
shoulders as she laid unconscious on the ground, in the middle of the lettered circle.

Katrina, you have a visitor. She opened her eyes and lifted herself out of her lumpy,
uncomfortable bed. Relieved she could leave her cell-like room and see her
husband.
The nurse opened her door and she walked alongside her down to the lobby area.
As she arrived she realised it was not her husband here to see her at all. Nope.
In his place was the nanny.

"What is she doing here?" Katrina asked, putting their walk to a halt.

"We believed it would be good for you to talk to her. Realise she isn't the person you thought she was. Show her how far you've come. Maybe then she will let your husband know how well you're doing and he will come to see you like he used to." The nurse replied, taking hold of her arm.

Katrina continued walking forward with the nurse to the middle of the lobby where Helen stood waiting for her. She looked straight ahead and into Helen's eyes, seeing only hatred and evil. There was no way she was here to help. Regardless, Katrina wanted them to see how well she was doing. She wanted to be back with her baby boy. She would do anything, even sit and talk with the Devil.

"Shall we go through to the activities lounge?" Helen asked Katrina in a child-like manner.
"Yes, let's." She replied with no emotion in her voice.

They headed back up the stairs, Helen led the way. Katrina walked behind her staring at the back of Helen's head and imagined throwing her over the bannister and running out the doors to be with her boy. Oh if only!

At the top of the stairs, they turned left and headed down the hall and into the activities room. This was where most visits took place, especially if you weren't trusted. Those who were trusted, were allowed to walk in the gardens and sit on the benches among the flowers looking out over the lake. Katrina, although seemingly doing better, was not trusted to be in the gardens.

Katrina sat in a chair by the window, her usual spot. She gazed out of the window at the others taking their visits in the gardens and having picnics by the water. She yearned to be outside in the sunshine, the rays kissing her pale, white skin.

"So the nurses say you've been improving?" Helen said to Katrina across the small coffee table.
"Why are you here Helen?" Katrina asked, her eyes not leaving the gardens.
"I thought you'd be glad of the company. Maybe let James know how you're doing."
"You mean Mr Taylor," Katrina said sternly, eyes now locked with Helens.
A small grin started to form on Helen's smug face, as if she knew that would wind her up.
"Yes of course.. Mr Taylor." She corrected herself with a smile and with her white, gloved hand picked up a small china cup of coffee and took a sip.

"I believe the treatments to be working well? The head doctor swears by them. You know, he's been in all the local newspapers this week?! He is becoming quite the legend."

"Is he?" Katrina replied coldly. How on earth could this man be made out as a hero, when he was torturing these poor souls. She could feel her blood start to boil at the thought of it.

"I wonder if he would think differently if it were himself being put through these god awful... treatments... as you call them." Katrina questioned.

"How dare you speak out of turn about the person helping you. Maybe you need longer in here than we thought." She threatened with raised eyebrows.

"No, maybe YOU need to be in here," Katrina argued. "You're the crazy one."

"Seems to me, everyone believes that you are the crazy one," Helen replied calmly, as she stood and crouched over so that she was head height with Katrina. She leaned in and whispered in her ear. "And my brother, the head of this amazing establishment, will see to it that you receive all the treatment you need."

Katrina stood up and shoved Helen backwards.

"Help! Help!" Helen cried out. "She's gone mad!"

"No, you're the mad one Helen! You're the devil! You just want me gone! You want my husband, you want my life!" Katrina screamed.

"I'll be speaking to Dr Watson about today's episode. He will help you darling. You will get through this. I'll make sure of it." Helen called out to her as the guards started to drag her away.

"You hear that?! She's threatening me and you're dragging ME away! What is wrong with you people? It's her who should be here, not me!" She screamed, as hot tears rolled down her cheeks.

"Please take me to see Dr Watson immediately," Helen demanded to a young nurse. The nurse didn't say anything, shy or scared... who knows. Either way, she did as she was told and led Helen back down the stairs and into the lobby.

"Please wait here." The nurse asked, as they stood next to the chairs in the reception area.

"I'll stand. He WILL see me, I can assure you." Helen insisted.

The nurse knocked on the office door.

"Come in." A hushed voice could be heard through the door.

"Ms Watson is here to see you regarding Mrs Taylor." She said politely.

"Of course send her in." He said, as he shuffled papers on his desk.

Helen barged past the nurse, looking down her nose at her and slammed the door in her face.

"Hello brother." Helen greeted as she walked up to his desk.

"What do you want now Helen? I'm busy." He moaned. " I have the Governor coming along later for a meeting and I have a lot of paperwork to sort before then." He continued.

"I want her gone," Helen demanded.

"She's stuck in here. She's already away from you. Why do you need her dead as well?" He asked, putting the papers down and lighting a cigarette.

"Oh Arthur. Do you forget the night I caught you having sex with a drugged up patient in the medicinal room?" She asked rhetorically. "I mean, was she even conscious?" she said as she leant down on the table with both hands, her head now the same height as his.

"What do you want me to do?" He asked shamefully, aware that if anyone were to find out about what he had done, he would be finished.

"I want you to kill her. You have all these medicines here. There must be something that you could give her that could slowly get rid of her without anyone noticing."

"Fine." He replied.

"Oh and while we're at it. I need more of that opium mixture." Helen added.

What happened to the last lot I gave you?" Arthur asked, annoyed with himself for letting a woman push him about. But there's nothing he could do without risking his reputation and career.

"She smashed the vile when she caught me pouring it into the baby's bottle." She informed him.

"Why can't you just leave this family alone?" He asked.

"Why don't you just hurry up and get my opium!" She demanded aggressively with her arms crossed.

He stood and strode over to the medicinal room, his white jacket floated behind him. He took a small silver key and slid it into the lock and twisted. He pulled the double doors open towards him and walked into the room.

It was a small room, but big enough to be caught doing the naughty it would seem. Shelves lined the walls from the floor to the ceiling and were full of all sorts of jars and bottles of tablets and liquids. He stepped up onto a stool and reached for the top shelf. He clutched a small bottle with pictures of angels on the front. He looked at the bottle, sighed and stepped back down.

Helen was right behind him as he turned around. He jumped back a little, startled to find her right there.

"This is the last time Helen." He declared, holding the bottle out to her.
She snatched it from his hand and walked away from him without saying a word, her heels tapped along the tiled floor in the medicinal room, until she reached the soft carpet of his office.
"I'll be back in a week." She turned to face him. "She better be gone," She growled, before walking out of the office and back to her carriage waiting outside for her.

A smell of menthol filled Abi's nose and she woke with a startle.
"It's okay, it's just us," Ben said, holding onto her hand gently. "You had another vision didn't you?" He asked sensitively.
"Yes." She said softly. "You're not going to believe this. You know when we got inside, we were in Doctor Watson's office?"
"Yeah..." Ben replied.
"Well... Doctor Watson seemed to be Helen's brother!"
"You've got to be joking!" Ben said, astonished. He got up and sat in a chair to the side.
"Wait, who is Helen again?" Jack asked.
"Now YOU have got to be kidding," Ben said frustrated.
"Yep!" Jack laughed.
"Okay, he's getting annoying now!" Abi said in anger, as she dusted herself off and stood up.
"Uh oh, did I say something," Jack asked with a big grin on his face.
"Did you say something?! YES, yes you did Jack. While Ben and I are taking things seriously and are here to get answers, you seem to think that it's okay to keep making jokes and acting like a complete twat!" Abi blurted, her anger bursting from within like a volcano erupting and spitting hot lava.
"Oh a twat am I?! Well sorry miss perfect for standing in your way, I guess I'll just leave you two love birds to it then shall I? I'll just get all my equipment back together and head off then!" He spat bitterly as he got closer to Abi.

Ben noticed a cold breeze enter the room and the temperature around them dropped dramatically.

"Hey guys knock it off. Does it feel cold in here to you?" Ben asked.

They didn't even seem to notice that he had said anything and continued to argue.
"Go on then. We don't need you. What information have you got us tonight huh? Oh yeah none.. I did!" She shouted at him.

The cold breeze that entered the room now flowed around Abi and Jack, still standing in the middle of the Ouija board. The breeze became faster and encircled them like a tornado sending papers flying around them, but they still didn't notice. It seemed the angrier they got, the faster the wind blew around them and the colder the room got.

Unable to get Abi and Jack to stop, he filmed the entire thing. He couldn't believe his eyes.

Jack stood in the centre with Abi shouting at him... but he didn't shout back anymore. He stood completely still, his shoulders started to hunch over slightly, his head bowed a little so his eyes were looking up towards his brow and the smile on his face seemed to stretch bigger and bigger. He no longer looked like himself. He looked evil. He started to chuckle lowly and got louder into a malevolent, bellowing laugh.

Abi realised what was happening and put her fear to the back of her mind, as this terrifying face got closer to her, she slapped him hard. The first slap seemed to do nothing but make whatever this entity was, angry.
Jack pushed Abi to the floor, knelt down and climbed on top of her.

Ben, just about able to see what was happening through the papers, books and other objects flying around them, dropped the camera and leaped into the whirlwind at Jack. They both went flying through the other side of the circling mayhem and he punched Jack square in the face, knocking him out.

The room fell silent and everything flying in the air, suddenly dropped to the ground with an almighty crash.

He chucked a bag on his back, picked Abi up off of the ground and held her in his arms. He rushed down the stairs, into the lobby and out the front door. He sat Abi down on the steps to get some air. He took the bag off his back, took a bottle of water from inside and handed it to Abi to drink.

"What the hell was that all about?!" He questioned out loud.
"I don't know," Abi replied shakily. "I felt so much rage towards him, I hated him so much. But that's not me Ben, I don't hate anyone!" She explained.
"I know it's not Abi. Something was affecting you both. Jack even more so though apparently. There's no way he would have done that Abi. He wouldn't hurt a fly. "

"I know. Whatever is in there is strong, Ben." She said in a scared voice. "We need to make sure Jack is okay."

"Yeah I know. Are you okay to come back in or do you want to stay out here for a bit?" He asked her.

"I'll come in with you. No way am I being anywhere on my own here." She insisted.

Ben held out his hand to her and helped her up.

They walked back into the lobby area.

The whole building seemed strangely quiet. They walked slowly up the stairs, their ears on high alert for any sounds of movement, but the place stayed silent. They headed back into the Ouija board room.

"Jack, are you okay?" Ben asked as they walked into the room.

He pointed the torch in the direction of where they had left him on the floor.

"Where is he?" Abi asked, a feeling of fear forming at the bottom of her gut.

He had vanished. They looked around the small room to see if he had just moved to another spot but no... he was gone.

"Jack?!" Ben shouted out.

No reply.

"Jack I know you didn't mean it. We were both being affected. It's okay!" Abi shouted after.

But still no reply.

"I don't have a good feeling about this Ben," Abi admitted.

"Me neither." He agreed.

"What should we do?" She asked him.

"Well, we have to try and find him. There's only two more rooms before the double doors in the hall. We should look in those rooms first. I have no idea what's beyond those two doors but we're going to find out."

Chapter 18

Ben and Abi collected the bags and equipment left in the Ouija room, leaving just one camera standing in the corner of the room and went in search of Jack.
They headed out of the door and into the gloomy, quiet hallway.
They walked into the room next door. It was filled with rubbish, blankets and smelled absolutely disgusting.
"People must have been staying in here." Ben guessed, covering his nose with his top. They got out sharpish and closed the door behind them.
"That smell has made me feel sick." Abi coughed, trying hard not to gag.

There was only one room left before the double doors and this room had no door. Just the old, white, chipped frame where once a door used to hang many years ago. Ben popped his head in and it was in a similar state to the last room they had been in. Empty beer cans scattered around the dirty, dusty floor. A smashed window with rusty iron bars... but still no sign of Jack.

Having run out of rooms to search in this area, it was time to go through the double doors waiting for them at the end of the hall.
Abi pushed on the left door and Ben the right. They pushed at the same time. Although they were swinging doors, where the building had been abandoned for so long, they were now stiff with age and heavy to push.

Once on the other side of the doors, the hallway went round to the left.
They followed it around. A long corridor ahead of them. No rooms. Windows lined the walls on both sides. One way looked out over the woodland on the outside of the Asylum and the other looked over gardens where a beautiful water feature sat in the middle.

Abi couldn't help but think of Katrina and how much she wanted to be outside in the gardens. She went up to a window to see more. She chose one that had seemed to have been smashed, as there was no longer any glass to fill it. She put her arm through the vacant window and shined the torch around. She saw one door on the opposite side with steps leading down to the garden.

"Hey Ben... Do you see that door on the other side?" She asked.
He pointed his torch in the same direction bringing more light to the location of the door and steps.
"Yeah?"
"Well remember when we walked up the stairs we couldn't turn left, could we? And I bet that's how you get to the gardens in the middle!" She exclaimed.
"Oh yeah! We'll have to see if there's another way to get there and check it out. But first, we need to find Jack. We can't just leave him behind and go searching for ghosts." He advised.
"Yeah I know. This place is so weird." She replied, looking down the long hall.

As they continued to walk, they saw another set of double doors.
As they reached them, they pushed the doors open hard, these doors even stiffer than the first set and this time, once Abi and Ben are through, the doors stayed stuck open.

On the other side they had two options, go left down another hall lined with doors, presumably more rooms... or go through the wooden door on their right.
Not wanting to choose which direction themselves. They flipped a coin.
Ben grabbed his wallet from his back pocket and took out a 50p coin.
"Heads its left, tails its right." He stated.
"Yep." Abi agreed.
He tossed it up in the air, caught it and placed it on top of his left hand. He pulled his right hand away revealing a 50p tail side up.
"Creepy door it is then!" Ben gulped.

Ben turned the cold metal knocker style handle on the dark, wooden door and pulled it open revealing a narrow, spiral staircase.

He took his first step onto the flagstone flooring in front of him, as Abi grabbed his hand.

"Wait. Does this not feel strange to you... like we've been here before, or that it's familiar for some reason?" Abi asked, feeling sick again.

"I don't know, maybe. We should check it out anyway. What if Jack is up here?" He replied.

They headed up the spiral stairs, holding onto a rope style handrail on the wall, just in case they tripped. They got to the top of the staircase and there was another door. Abi was feeling really strange and couldn't explain why. Ben pushed the door open.

A library stood before them.

They walked slowly into the room.

"Erm... Abi... Have you been here before?" He asked as he took in their surroundings. "This looks just like YOUR library!" He announced.

Abi stood there in disbelief. She had never been here before, so why was this library and her own almost identical?!

"No! Never! This is freaky." She declared. A solitary tear escaped down her cheek in fear.

"I don't like this Ben. I want to leave."

"We can't leave yet though. We've not got any answers and Jack is still missing."

A low moan can be heard on the other side of the room. Abi grabbed Ben's arm.

He moved the torch slowly in the direction of the creepy sound.

"Jack!" Ben shouted across the room.

They both ran over to him. Jack laid there, curled up with his head in his hands. He looked terrified, like a small child frightened by the dark.

"Jack, are you okay? What happened? We've been looking everywhere for you!" Ben exclaimed.

"I don't know. I just woke up here. What happened? I remember standing with Abi in the Ouija board circle but then it's just blank." Jack questioned.

"You were both arguing, like really badly. Stuff was flying up around you both. Something was seriously messing with you both, especially you. Your whole demeanour changed and you got aggressive, but you were happy about it. Your face was really strange and you wouldn't stop laughing." Ben explained to him.

"Oh, I... I don't remember any of that," Jack replied.

There was a strange look in his eyes. Something unexplainable.

There seemed to be a black dot in his eye where there wasn't before. Ben shrugged it off, maybe he just never noticed it before.

"Well, how are you feeling? Can you carry on or do you want out?" He asked Jack.
"I'm all good. You know I wouldn't hurt Katrina right?" Jack replied.
"You mean Abi?" Ben said in confusion.
"Yeah, you know what I mean."

Ben helped Jack to his feet and his eyes darted straight to Abi as he stood. She took a few steps back, clearly not completely trusting him as before.
"Alright Abi?" He asked her with a smile.
"Yep. You?" she replied bluntly.
"Yeah, that must have been insane right?!" He said, his smile even more so unnerving.
"Yeah. Insane. Now can we get out of here please. I'm not comfortable being in this room." She pleaded.
"Why? What's wrong with this room?" Jack asked, looking around the library.
"Uh, have you not seen this place? Do you not think it looks just like MY library?" She said sarcastically.
"Hmm, yeah I suppose... if you say so," he replied. His expression in his eyes was completely blank but his smile remained.

Abi stepped back further.

"Ben, he is acting strange. I don't believe that is Jack." Abi admitted.
"Don't be silly Abi, of course, it's me." He said as he stepped towards her.
"Okay, prove it's you. Tell me one thing only you and I would know." Ben challenged him.
"Okay. What about that night in the treehouse... we were 17. Your mum thought you were at Callum's house as she didn't want you hanging around with 'a nobody' like me. She wanted you to be around educated people, not working-class like me. We went out that night, being young and stupid, I stole a bottle of Jager, you got someone to buy us cigarettes and we headed to the woods to our secret treehouse." Jack said.
"Abi, it's him. No one else knows about the treehouse. And my mum hated Jack with a passion." Ben convinced her.
"Okay, but I don't want to be left around him anymore. I'm sorry." She apologised.
"If he gets taken over again, I don't want him anywhere near me, who knows what he's capable of when he's not himself." She worried.
"That's fine. Agreed Jack?" He asked.
"Yeah... Agreed." He said in a strange voice.

The Woman In The Mirror

"Right, now that's settled, let's get back downstairs. We still have lots of areas to investigate." Jack instructed, he didn't notice the small change in Jack's voice.
"Fine by me, this place gives me the creeps." She admitted again, happy to get out of there as quickly as possible.

They headed back down the stairs and out into the hallway. They started walking down the hall and came to the first room. The door opened, revealing an empty room with just one rocking chair sitting in the middle.
"Well I'm not going in there!" Abi cried. "You two can, I'll wait out here by the door, I can film from here and see if I can capture anything on camera." She suggested.
"Yeah okay, Jack, why don't you take the camera, you are the professional," Ben said to Jack.
"I sure am." He said ,as he snatched the camera from him in a hurry and strode into the room.
"Anybody here?!" He shouted out, as he wandered around the room in a circle.
"Ben, please tell me you can sense it too. He's not right." She whispered to Ben, who still stood by her at the door.
"I did knock him out, Abi. Maybe I gave him a bit of concussion. At this point we have to give him the benefit of the doubt." He assured her. But he didn't really assure her of anything.
Abi stuck with her gut feeling, whether Ben could see it or not, she would not be convinced otherwise.

Ben headed into the room holding onto the spirit box.
In a more sensible manner than Jack's approach, he called out. "Are there any spirits in our presence? We would like to speak to you. Speak into this little box in my hand and we will hear what you say."
"She is here." A voice came through the box.
Ben and Abi looked directly into each other's eyes in shock.
"Who is here?" Ben called out in reply.
The device flicked through multiple radio stations and white noise until another word came through.
"Evil."

Jack laughed menacingly.

"Well that's not funny is it!" Ben snapped at Jack. "Something here is evil and it could be whatever or whoever messed with you both in the Ouija room."

A strange rhythmic squeaking noise came from behind them in the middle of the dark empty room.

They turned around slowly and noticed the old rocking chair moving gently back and forth, as if someone was sitting in it and rocking slowly. Every forward and backward motion gave an eerie creaking noise as it moved.

"Garden." A muffled voice came through the box randomly, making Ben and Abi jump out of their skins, the chair still rocking gently.

"The garden?" Abi questioned. "The garden! " She exclaimed."In my vision, Katrina wanted to be in the gardens but she wasn't trusted. What if that's Katrina trying to come through on the spirit box?!" She asked anxiously.

"Katrina is that you?" Ben asked.

The spirit box stayed silent.

"Ohh Katrina?!" Jack called as if taunting her.

"I'm getting sick of you." Abi hissed at Jack.

He just laughed in reply.

"Don't start you two. We should try and find a way into the gardens." Ben suggested.

"The obvious way to the gardens is through that doorway at the top of the stairs, but of course, it's been bricked up. We will have to find another way in." Abi commented.

"What if we COULD get through that way?" Jack hinted.

"What do you mean Jack?" Abi huffed.

"What if we could get through that doorway? I have a feeling we could get through it." Jack replied.

"What are you going to do, get your wand out and magic it away?" She replied sarcastically.

Jack walked off back through the double doors, leaving Ben and Abi behind him in the darkness.

"Well we can't just let him wander off, quick we have to stay together," Ben said urgently.

They headed back through the 2 sets of double doors and back onto the balcony overlooking the lobby area.

Jack approached the bricked up doorway and pushed the left side of it. It wasn't bricked up at all! It was a disguised doorway! But why? Why would this wing be blocked off like this?

115

The heavy door scratched the floor as it slid open away from them, disturbing the dirt on the floor and dust particles flying up into the air, highlighted by their torches.
"Come on then," Jack said.
Ben and Abi look at each other confused. How did Jack know about the door? He seemed so blasé about it, as if everyone was meant to know it was there.

They followed him through the door into the west wing of the asylum.

Strangely, this part of the building had no dust, no dirt, no rubbish or broken tiles on the floor. It looked as though someone had been cleaning it regularly. As they stepped in, they noticed a wine coloured carpet beneath their feet and a warmness in the atmosphere. Whilst they looked down at the carpet as they walked in, they saw sun rays falling on the floor from the large windows lining the hallway.
Abi and Ben looked up at each other in confusion.

"What's going on?" Ben asked Abi with a frown across his brows.
"I have no idea," Abi replied, looking back through the door into the darkness of the main building. "It's strange, It feels like one of my visions... but I'm awake... WE'RE awake." She exclaimed.

Jack had wandered off, AGAIN, leaving Abi and Ben in their confusion.

Abi started walking down the hall with Ben and looked out through the window into the gardens. It seemed to be a bright, sunny winters day. The windows were slightly open to let in a fresh, cool breeze. The windows didn't seem to open more than a few centimetres. Presumably for the safety of the patients. They heard the birds singing in the garden and cleaning themselves in the beautiful, circular fountain in the middle of the garden, the waters flowing and sparkling in the sunlight.

A male nurse stood alone in the gardens, next to the fountain with a look of concern upon his face. He paced back and forth then looked up to the windows. Abi could see a lady standing at the window in the next hallway, almost like a reflection of herself.
"Katrina!" Abi called out.
They both ran along the hallway, in the direction of where they saw Katrina. Through the first set of double doors and... Darkness.

"What the hell is going on?!" Ben questioned, agitated.
"Wait! Let's go back through the doors." Abi suggested.

They headed back through the doors where they had been only seconds ago in warm daylight.

No change.

The hallway that had just been filled with a fresh breeze and warm, sunny rays, was now in complete darkness, just as the rest of the building was. Clean, wine carpet now in tatters and filled with dust and dirt. Broken windows and graffiti walls. A silence filled the air, replacing the sweet singing of the birds playing in the fountain in the gardens below.

"This is so strange. Why would we both get a vision and then it disappear right in front of our eyes?" She asked. Her brows tightened. "What are we missing?"

"Didn't you say a man was trying to help Katrina in one of your visions? What if that was the man trying to help her down in the gardens? And what we saw wasn't a vision but a time loop?" Ben suggested excitedly.

"Of course! Yes!" She exclaimed. "He wanted to help her escape. But what do you mean, time loop?"

"It's something Jack has mentioned before when he has done other investigations. Sometimes, instead of spirits moving on, they either stick around due to unfinished business or they get stuck in a time loop, like an old memory playing over and over again, stuck in time."

"Interesting. Speaking of Jack... He's done a disappearing act again Ben. I told you something wasn't right with him. If he was back to normal, why would he just wander off like that and leave us here?"

"I don't know. I'm sorry, I should have listened to you." He apologised.

From within the dark silence, a patter of footsteps seemed to run fast behind them and the lights above their heads started to flash.

They both spun around to check behind them with their torches, but there was no one to be seen. They turned back around facing the hall.

They noticed a small, blacker than black shadow at the end of the hall, where they had first entered the west wing.

It was crouched down on all fours, like an animal. A long drip of saliva slithering down from the wide-open mouth, its jaw seemingly jammed open.

Its long, thin limbs were holding it up like a gigantic, house spider. The creature's head looked at them and twisted slowly to the right, while its glowing, yellow eyes maintained eye contact with them.

A strong smell of urine filled the air.

The creature spread its limbs out and stood up on two legs, revealing that it wasn't a creature at all, but a long, skinny woman in a pale, white nightgown.

117

Ben and Abi remained frozen to the spot. Abi found Ben's hand with her fingers and held it tightly. A bead of sweat rolled down Ben's forehead and past the corner of his eye. He took a big gulp and at the sound of saliva being forced down his throat, the figure started to slowly move towards them.

As the old woman stepped forward into the flickering lights, they could make out her long, grey, straw-like hair, two dark holes where her eyes should have been and little yellow dots in place of pupils. Her face was as grey as her hair.

Her mouth opened impossibly wider, showing a cave-like hole widening larger and larger until sharp, loud screams bellowed from deep within her, shattering any remaining windows and started lunging towards them, her long legs getting lankier by the second,

Abi screamed and they finally ran for their lives through the double doors.
They headed around the corner in the direction of where they saw Katrina. More dark, empty rooms lined the hallway. They ran into the second room as the door was already wide open. They got in as fast as they could, shut the door behind them and leant up against the walls beside it in hopes that, that THING wouldn't see them through the small window of the paint chipped, wooden door and go in after them.

The woman drifted from door to door as if trying to sniff them out, zig-zagging across the old corridor.
The woman's face appeared at the small window. Only her eyes could be seen glowing through the dirty glass.

"Katrinaaa." The voice hissed lowly through the door.

Abi shut her eyes tight and clenched her jaw shut. A tear fell down her cold cheek. She breathed out slowly and her breath became a visible cloud in front of her mouth.
The room turned ice cold and she became lightheaded.
The room around her swayed like a boat on the ocean and before she had a chance to grab anything, she fell to the floor with a loud thud as her head hit the ground.

The spindly woman-like thing, once on the other side of the door, was nowhere to be seen.

Ben rushed down to where Abi laid unconscious on the cold stone floor.

"Where the heck are you Jack?!" Ben questioned angrily.

"Oh Abi, I'm so sorry." He whispered, as he lifted her head gently onto his lap and placed his jacket over her to keep her warm.

"I wish there was more I could do to help," he said, full of guilt as he swept a stray hair from her face.

He watched over Abi while she appeared to be sleeping. Her breath was shallow and her chest barely moved.

He heard footsteps slowly walking along the corridor.

Pat. Pat. Pat. Pat.

"That better be you Jack." He huffed silently.

He pulled the bag from his back, placed it underneath Abi's head as support and stood up.

He edged slowly towards the door and looked out of the murky window, into the dark, gloomy hallway.

The hall remained still, with no one in sight.

He turned the rusty brass knob on the door, pulled it gently open and stepped out into the darkness leaving the door open behind him.

He shined his torch down each end of the hall, but couldn't explain the phantom footsteps he had heard only moments before.

A dragging noise appeared right behind him and just as he noticed what it was, the door to the room where Abi lay sleeping, slammed shut behind him.

The loud bang echoed down the empty hall.

Chapter 19

Abi floated above her body in a daze. Laying in the air, parallel to her own body, she was staring down at herself.
She turned her head to look at her arm stretched out beside her and wondered in amazement as she moved her fingers slowly through the air.
She brought herself to the ground so that she was standing next to her body.

The room seemed to look different, almost as if she was wearing tinted glasses that made colours seem dull and faded.

She looked around the room. Ben was sitting with her body and moving her head onto his lap.
"Well at least I'm still alive." She said out loud as she watched the slow rising and falling of her chest.

She felt a cold chill come over her and a green fog came from behind her.
She spun around to find green smoke flooding out onto the floor from a huge silver framed mirror that had appeared on the flaky wall.
"Well, you weren't there before." She whispered to the mirror.
She walked slowly towards it and as she stepped closer she saw a figure in the mirror, staring straight back at her and seemingly getting larger as if it was her own reflection.

But this wasn't her reflection.

The expression on the reflection's face was that of fear and sadness. Not what Abi was feeling at all. She felt excited, light. She could feel what felt like adrenalin, but was unsure how as she was no longer in her body. It was like she was made of electricity and she could feel the energy in her fingers, almost like pins and needles, as if she were to give someone a shock if she touched them.

She moved closer to the mirror and finally stood directly in front of it, the emerald smoke floating around her feet.
Katrina!
She could see that Katrina was mouthing words, but could not hear anything she was trying to say.
"I can't hear you!" Abi exclaimed loudly, pointing to her mouth in hopes Katrina would realise.

Katrina stopped.
Tears swelled in her eyes, she slowly lifted her hand and placed it on the glass in front of her.
"Help" Katrina mouthed.

This time Abi could read her lips and what she was trying to say.

She looked at her own hands and feeling compelled, she lifted her hand and matched Katrina's on the mirror, her fingertips touching the cold glass first and then her palm.
The mirror fogged up and seemed to start dripping with water.

A bright light flashed and blinded her for a second. She scrunched her eyes up tight and whipped her hands away from the mirror to cover her eyes.

After a few seconds, she took her hands away slowly and squinted through the slowly dimming light.

The mirror was no longer in front of her and she was now outside in the gardens. The sound of birds singing filled the frosty, November breeze that flowed through the strands of her thick, auburn waves.

She was sitting on the cold, marble wall of the fountain in the middle of the grounds in her white, plain gown, shivering from the snowflakes that had fallen on her snow-white skin. She felt as if she was waiting for someone. The grounds were completely empty. She could hear singing from one of the rooms above, where the rest of the patients were involved with a music class.

It was this time of day that classes were held and activities to keep the patients busy were being undertaken. Today it was a choice between music, painting or yoga. Katrina had made sure that she couldn't be involved with today's activities by starting an argument at breakfast with another patient. It had felt cruel to upset another patient like that, but what other choice did she have.

The day before, the young security man had managed to get her alone to put a plan together to get her out of this horrible place. He saw Katrina for who she really was and wanted to take her as far away from here as he could and her son with them too.

They agreed that she would make a scene, so that she would miss out on the activities. That way she would be made to stay in her room and all the staff would be busy with the patients in the activity rooms and hall. While the staff were busy, he would slip a key under the door and head to the back storage room where they keep all the clothes that the patients arrive in.

He packed her belongings into a bag and started to make his way to the gardens where they had agreed to meet.

He made his way down the corridor. Beautiful sunlight flooded in through the frosted windows giving him a spring in his step... that was until he heard nurses ahead of him talking and their footsteps coming in his direction.
With Katrina's bag in his hand, he could not afford for them to see him. He quickly slipped into one of the patient's rooms, but as he shut the door behind him, it shut a bit too hard and made a clanging noise that echoed down the hall.

Both nurses turned their heads sharply in the direction of the loud, metal clang.
"Who's there?!" The head nurse shouted out rather demandingly, her voice unexpectedly deep.
She was tall, her blonde locks pinned up with a few curls dangling freely, framing her blemish-free, perfectly featured face and a white nurse's hat upon her head.
"Everyone should be taking part in their classes and anyone found to be abandoning their duties will be punished." She exclaimed strictly.

He quickly flung the bag under the bed and pulled the door back open and stepped out into the hall.

"It's only me ladies. Just doing my daily room checks for any prohibited items." He claimed, as he pulled his keys from his pocket and locked the door behind him. They gave him a quizzical look, as if they didn't believe him.

"Would you ladies like to recheck or can I continue with my duties?" He asked. as he stepped towards the next room. His heart rate went through the roof and he could feel his palms getting clammy as he waited for their response. If the nurses decided to call his bluff and check the room, they would find the bag and their plan would be ruined.

"Carry on." The other said, looking him up and down. She was quite the opposite of the other nurse. This one was short and plump and quite scruffy for a nurse. Her hair looked knotted and her face shiny from excess oil.

The two nurses continued to walk towards him, but their eyes didn't leave his until they had passed him. The one closest to the door, stopped and glanced into the room through the door window.

He jangled his keys and started to open the door to the neighbouring room, acting as though he was working his way through the rooms and carrying out his daily checks.

The tall nurse turned to look at him as he turned the key in the lock.

"If you're up to something I will find out. And when I do, you'll be gone." She threatened with a smirk, before turning on her heels and walking away.

With these words, he imagined every school girl bully. Thinking she was above everyone else and everyone should be kissing her feet. Typical bully.
"She must have had a lot of home issues to turn out as nasty as she did." He thought.
How could someone like that be given a job as a nurse? Nurses are meant to be caring, but she certainly did not seem that way.

He waited for them to turn the corner and their echoing footsteps to be out of hearing range. He closed his eyes, his hand still holding the key in the door's lock, listening closely for any sounds of people nearby.

He blew a big, deep breath out in relief and headed back to the room where he had stored the getaway bag. He unlocked the door and pushed it open making a loud, high pitched screech as it swayed open into the room. He knelt by the bed and grabbed the bag.

As he placed his hand on the bag he could feel eyes staring at him, a presence behind him. He looked around quickly, facing the door to the room, but there was no one there.

He pulled the bag out from under the bed. Now covered in dust and dirt, he started giving it a shake and pat to clean it off before heading back out the door.

He approached the door but held back slightly, listening again for any movements outside of the room. Happy with the silence, he slowly popped his head out into the hallway looking both left and right before closing the door behind him and locking it for the final time.

He trod carefully into the corridor and took the next turn to where the stairs to the garden are located. He looked out of the window and saw Katrina sitting by the still, un-flowing fountain waiting for him. He stared in a daze, the sound of birds singing in the snowy gardens and brisk breeze coming through a crack in the window.

The sound of freedom.

All of a sudden, anxiety fell in the pit of his stomach, sickness brewing and dread and fear swirling.

Something was wrong.

He looked around, up and down the hallways and through the nearby windows.

No-one.

"Pull yourself together man." He said to himself quietly.

He took a deep breath and pushed the handle down on the door and stepped out into the icy air, onto the top step.

Katrina looked up at him as she heard him step out onto the metal steps leading down to the gardens. A soft smile stretched across her face in relief that he had turned up.

She was so nervous that he would have been caught and their plan to leave and escape together would be ruined.

He walked carefully down the steps, trying not to cause any attention from sudden loud noises. All he wanted to do was run as fast as he could down to her, grab her in his arms tight and run far away as quick as possible. But he knew that he would just be putting them both in trouble by causing that amount of noise.

"Stay calm, almost there." He whispered to himself, as he took step by step as quietly as he could.

Near the last steps, he couldn't hold himself back any longer and jumped the last few and onto the fresh, glistening snow and ran up to Katrina taking her in his arms and holding her close, snowflakes settling in their hair.
Still holding her in his arms, he said in a quiet voice to her, " I have your clothes in the bag, but we need to get out of here first and get as far away as possible."

"Oh is that so?" A familiar voice called out.

They both looked up at the stairs. The head nurse!

He grabbed the bag with one hand and Katrina's hand in the other and they ran in the opposite direction towards the arch that led to the outside grounds. Their escape.
Their pulses rushed and their breaths were short and fast. They approached the arch and the assistant nurse came out of nowhere, now standing in the middle of the archway, blocking their exit.

"You're not going anywhere!" The head nurse called out, sounding more than happy with herself.
"You were following me this whole time weren't you Margaret?" He asked angrily.
"But of course!" She gloated. "I knew you were up to something and I told you I would find out. You really thought you would get away with this? What, you thought you were going to run away and live happily ever after did you Thomas? Ha!"

She pulled a whistle from inside her blouse and blew.
A sharp, loud noise came screaming from the whistle, alerting all of the staff and the siren alarmed through the halls, rooms and gardens. Staff flooded the grounds around them and patients were hurried back to their rooms and locked away whilst the hospital director, Dr Arthur Watson, was summoned to deal with Thomas and Katrina.

A circle of security men and nurses surrounded them in the snow. Thomas, Katrina and Margaret stood in the middle.
The sirens fell silent leaving only the sounds of nature around them. Not a word or a mumble from anyone.

Clang, clang, clang.

Dr Wilson started walking down the metal steps, his shoes creating a loud clang with every step he took. His gloved hand glided down the rail as he reached the last step and marched over to stand next to Nurse Davies.

"Well, well, well. What is going on here then Nurse Davies?" Dr Watson asked, a small pair of glasses sitting on the edge of his nose, dressed in a black suit and black hat, the rim of which protected his eyes from the low winter sun.
"It seems Mr Andrews and Mrs Taylor were trying to run away together. Not only is Mrs Taylor still meant to be having treatments for her insanity, but now it is obvious she was also committing adultery."
"Well we can't have that now can we Nurse Davies. Mr Andrews, you will no longer be working for us at Blue Waters hospital. You will hand in your uniform right away and be escorted from the premises by REAL security men, who take their jobs seriously."
"You will never get away with how you treat people here. I will make sure that everyone knows what kind of hospital you are running here and the torture you put innocent people through!" Thomas threatened, as two security men took each of his arms.
"Take him to my office and retrieve his uniform. He doesn't leave the premises until I have had my last words with him." He demanded the two security men.

They tried to force him to walk by kicking the back of his knee and dragged him away from Katrina.

"I will get you away from here Katrina! I promise!" He called out, his feet left drag marks in the snow from being pulled away.

"Now what do you suppose we do with Mrs Taylor, Nurse Davies?" Dr Watson asked.
"Well she is due her next set of treatment, but Mr Taylor was meant to be arriving this afternoon too for visitation." She replied.
"Well see if Mr Taylor can come in earlier for his visit and advise him that there has been a situation.."
"NO!" Katrina begged before he could finish his sentence.
"What do you mean no?! How dare you interrupt me." Dr Watson replied, angered at her outburst.
"Please, don't tell him I was going to run away with Mr Andrews. I will do as I'm told and I won't complain about the treatments, I promise. Just please don't tell James,

please. I beg you." Katrina pleaded, her knees fell down into the snow beneath her as she begged.

"Fine."

"But.." Nurse Davies started.

"But just this once and Nurse Davies here will be putting you through your treatment herself after the visit. We will cure you of this madness in your brain. You will only have interaction with female nurses, so that we can assure that no other men hinder your progress."

"Thank you, thank you so much." She cried, her head falling at his feet and tears started falling down her cheeks and melting the snow as they dropped.

Dr Watson turned and walked back in the direction of the stairs, his feet making crunching noises in the snow as he walked away.

"But Dr Watson.." Nurse Davies called out as she started walking to catch up with him.

"No buts Nurse Davies. Do your job." He looked over his shoulder at her. "Unless you'd like to be demoted. I'm sure one of these lovely staff members would love to take your job and wages. Now go and get her freshened up for her visit with Mr Taylor."

Nurse Taylor stopped immediately in her tracks.

"Yes sir. Sorry sir." She replied. Her hands rolled into fists behind her back in anger.

She turned slowly and looked straight at Katrina, still laying in the snow crying. The rest of the staff all headed back inside to carry on with their daily duties.

"Right." Nurse Davies said, walking back towards Katrina. "Stand up! I've had enough of the trouble you cause. We will get this visit done and tonight I am stomping this behaviour out! I will cure you and get you out of here myself. I've had enough of dealing with you. Your husband can take you to another hospital once I let you go." She grabbed Katrina's arm tightly and yanked her up aggressively, but she slipped on the ice and fell back into the cold, wet snow.

"Come on!" She shouted at Katrina, as if she did it on purpose just to stall them.

She climbed back up, holding onto the icy wall of the fountain to steady herself as she pulled herself up.

Her dress was soaked through and her skin was burning from the cold November snow.

"I am not a troublemaker." She stated as she steadied herself. "You choose to believe I am wrong and punish me for speaking the truth. Why do you not believe me?"

"Why would your husband lie, Katrina?! He is a self-made, respectful man. He has no reason to lie. Now get inside." She demanded.

"But that's just it isn't it? Men are seen to be above all and respected, but we as women have to obey them or we are in the wrong, right? Just like when Dr Watson threatened you with your job, so you had to do as the man told you, otherwise you're in the wrong."

"THAT'S ENOUGH!" Nurse Davies shouted at her, coming to a complete stop. She turned around, stormed toward Katrina and slapped her so hard around the face that it left a stinging, red handprint on her pale white skin.

"And if anyone asks, you were hysterical and I had to smack you out of it for your own good. NOW GET MOVING!" She grabbed her arm and pushed Katrina forward in front of her.

Katrina stumbled forward and nearly fell back into the snow, but caught her balance just in time. She walked slowly over to the metal staircase to the hospital west wing, her dress dragged heavily through the thick snow.

She weightfully climbed the cold, slippery steps to the first-floor entrance from the gardens, looking back over her shoulder, down to where she nearly escaped as hot tears trickled down her icy cheeks.

The head nurse pushed Katrina forward and marched her back to the washrooms.

The washrooms smelt damp. Black mould surrounded the edges of the small, rectangle windows that let light into the room. The old pipes dripped continuously, sending cold droplets of water onto the already soaked tiled floor.

Katrina walked to the back of the room where the head nurse began to shower her. Katrina was not given the privilege of washing alone with warm water. She would not be allowed to be on her own now, until she showed improvement in her actions. She looked up to the showerhead above her as a single drop of water hit her forehead, followed by a rush of freezing water.
She didn't know what was worse. The snow or the shower!
She let out a loud shriek as the water attacked her skin.

After a quick wash, Nurse Davies threw a towel at Katrina who was standing there dripping wet and shivering from the cold.

"You'll soon warm up." She said dismissively and turned towards the door.
"Come on then, your Husband will be here soon."
Katrina followed the nurse out of the door and down the hallway, still shivering in her towel.

As she walked down the corridor, leaving watery footprints behind her, sniggers, cackles and pointed fingers came at her from behind the closed doors that she passed along the way.

She finally reached her own room and slowly walked in and sat on her bed.
"Get dressed." Nurse Davies demanded as she threw a change of clothes onto the bed next to her.
"I'll be back in 30 minutes to collect you for your visit."
She took the keys from her pocket, closed the door behind her as she walked out and turned the key until it clicked.

Katrina waited for the footsteps to fade and then burst. She collapsed into her pillow and screamed muffled screams through the feather innards. Crying until she couldn't cry anymore. Her throat grew sore and her head throbbed as she lifted herself back up from the tear-soaked cushion.
She placed her head in her hands and regained her breath.
"Why are they doing this to me?" she whispered to herself. "I'll show them."
I will get out of here. They don't have to know what I'm really thinking. But I will make sure I get out. I will do what they say. If they want me to be BETTER, then I will show them exactly what they want to see.

She stood up, changed into a dress identical to the plain white one she was wearing earlier in the day and popped a beige knitted cardigan over the top for warmth. At least they allowed her that.

She heard the familiar click of the lock and the door swung open.
"Visiting time. You will have 30 minutes and then it's time for your therapy."
"Yes ma'am," Katrina replied politely.
She walked toward the head nurse and waited outside of the room whilst Nurse Davies locked the door once more.
They walked together down the corridor and into the visitor's hall where James was waiting in an armchair by the window. His glasses sat on the edge of his nose whilst he read the latest newspaper.
Nurse Davies stood at the door whilst Katrina strode towards her husband.

"Hello James." She said warmly. "It's so lovely for you to visit." A warm smile on her soft face.

"Yes, indeed." He replied plainly. "You look... well."

"Thank you. It's the cold showers. They do wonders for your skin."

"Well, you sound as though you are finally starting to get better. How have the therapies been? I hear that Dr Watson has some groundbreaking therapies. He is becoming quite renowned."

"Oh yes, I do believe they have been working wonders for me. Hopefully, I am able to return home to you and little George soon. How is he?" She asked, a lump started to form in her throat as tears threatened her eyes.

"He is doing well. Helen is making sure that he grows big and strong while I am working."

Just the sound of her name coming from his lips made her hairs stand on end and her fingernails dig deep into her palms as she held in her anger.

"Is that so?" She replied. "I am so glad. I do miss him. And you. I do look forward to taking him to the park again to feed the ducks. He loved seeing the ducks."

"Yes he does. Helen takes him regularly."

She could feel her blood start to boil and right now, she didn't want to be anywhere near him. Anything to get away from him and the vile words coming out of his mouth. It made her feel sick to her stomach that Helen of all people was looking after her baby.

"Oh good, I'd hate for him to miss out whilst I'm here. I hope she is wrapping him up warm. The snow is freezing."

"Oh, you have been out, have you?" He asked, sounding a little surprised.

"Yes but only this morning. Just a small time in the garden with the head nurse." She replied.

Well she wasn't one hundred percent lying now was she.

"Speaking of which, I have another therapy session to attend and if I want to get better, I best not delay. The sooner I am better, the sooner we can be a family again." She said as she stood from the table.

"Well good luck with your recovery and I will schedule another visit soon."

"Thank you again James." She squeezed his hand and walked back in the direction of Nurse Davies who was still standing, waiting by the door for her.

"You still have 10 minutes left." She said, surprised that Katrina had ended their visit early.

"You know we will be going to the therapy room now don't you?"

"Yes, I know." She replied softly, her head dropped to face the floor as she walked into the corridor.

She walked side by side with the nurse, through the corridor to the therapy room. As they approached the therapy room door, the same green smoke from the mirror started to flood out from underneath the entrance.

Nurse Davies didn't seem to notice and continued towards the door.

The smoke was so thick that Katrina could no longer see the door, but saw Nurse Davies disappear into it and followed.

She passed through the smoke and was back on the other side of the mirror.

Abi turned around quickly and Katrina stood there looking back at her through the mirror, both surrounded by a thick green fog and she slowly faded away.

Chapter 20

Katrina faded in front of Abi's eyes, leaving just her reflection looking back at her from the antique framed mirror before her.
The reflection not only showed herself, but also her body laying on the stone floor behind her, debris scattered around the room. The floor had seemed to have cracked and crumbled over the many years that the building had been left unaccompanied.

One thing standing out more than the rest though, was that Ben didn't seem to be beside her body where she had left him.

She turned around and scanned the room, but he was nowhere to be seen.
She didn't have a good feeling at this point. A feeling of dread came over her and she felt sick to her stomach.
"I need to find Ben," she whispered to herself, looking back down upon her own body lying there on the floor.

She glided towards her body and as she got close, she noticed glass around her and goosebumps appeared, tingling on her skin.
It was not just glass though. After taking a closer look she noticed they were dirty shards of mirror.
As she scanned them she noticed a shadow in one. Not believing her eyes, she slowly turned around and looked up into the corner of the ceiling where the shadow had been seen in the broken piece of mirror.

There, before her eyes, a huge black mass spreaded from the corner of the ceiling, growing and from the middle of it, she could see two red eyes.

"Katriiinnnaa." A voice called in a hushed, malevolent tone.
"I am not Katrina!" She shouted back at the mass, which was starting to take human form.

She quickly turned back to her body and climbed back into her mortal shell.

Feeling a little light-headed, she opened her eyes slowly and the once shadowy form in the corner of the ceiling had now formed into a woman. Almost completely transparent, but you could see that she was in a nurse's uniform, her hair pinned back with a hat upon her head.

The figure lingered right over her face where she still lay on the cold, stone floor. Staying as still as she possibly could, her own eyes stared straight into the figures. Above her.
The entity's eyes however, were completely different and inhumane, unlike the rest of the formed body. It was like staring into deep black tunnels that led to the fiery pits of hell.

As she laid there staring back at this thing, she found her head getting tighter and tighter until it felt like it was going to explode.
She screamed the most deathly of screams that seemed to echo throughout the whole building.

"Abi!" Ben shouted from the other side of the door.
He banged his fists hard against the wooden door, it shook with every thud from his fists, but refused to give way.

Abi felt like her head was about to explode. She started to notice a white light to the side of her. All of a sudden the door swung open and Ben came charging in as he took a run-up to the door, obviously not expecting it to have opened as he ran towards it and ran straight through the shadowy nurse, hitting the wall opposite with full force.
Instead of falling to the floor as you would expect, he fell straight through the wall leaving it in a crumbly mess.

The dust and rock that filled the space, started to drift and settle to the ground exposing a hidden room. No doors, no windows. It was pitch black, like he had fallen into a void of nothingness.

"Ben, Ben are you okay?" Abi cried out as she pulled herself across the floor, to the new opening in the wall.
Ben coughed as he came back into consciousness.
"Yep." he coughed again, "I'm fine."
Abi pulled herself up and climbed over the debris of the wall, being careful not to trip.
She moved some of the stone and reached for the torch from beneath the rubble.
She aimed it into the room to find Ben, but instead the light shone right back at her. She blinded herself for a few moments, before she realised the walls inside the room were floor to ceiling mirrors.
She stepped inside the room to join Ben and waved the torch around the room. Every wall was a mirror. So many mirrors. The room was made hexagonal, so everywhere they looked, they were surrounded by more versions of themselves.

Abi held out her hand to help Ben up from the dusty, rubble covered floor.
"Where the hell are we?" Ben asked, still coughing from the dust that was trapped in his throat.

"I'm not sure." She replied, as she walked up to the mirrors.
She slowly edged towards one of the mirror walls and gently placed her finger onto the surface. As her fingertip pressed against the glass surface, it turned to water beneath her touch and sent ripples across all the other walls.

"Ben, I think we need to go through." She said, brushing her hand along the surface.
"When I was unconscious, I left my body and went through a mirror. I became Katrina and learnt more about her. That thing you just ran through was the head nurse, or at least on of the nurses. What if there are secrets through there that? Secrets they're trying to hide?"
"Exactly, what if there are secrets they are trying to keep and will do anything to keep you from finding them out Abi?" Concern in his voice.
"Abi, what if you get seriously hurt? As you've said, you've already passed out once and that THING came after you! What if I hadn't made it into the room Abi? What then?"
"I'm okay though Ben. Look how far we've come"
"Yeah and what if going through there is the end of it Abi?"

"I can't just give up now. We've come so far and gone through so much. It would all be for nothing if we go home now. I feel like we are so close to getting all of our answers, Ben. Please don't give up on me now, please?" Abi Begged.

"Abi.."

"Please Ben?"

"Fine! But if we don't find anything or you're in danger again, we are leaving."

"Absolutely! Thank you Ben." She said, putting her hand out as if to ask him to hold it.

He took her hand and they both headed towards the mirrors, hand in hand. They take one final look at each other. Abi could feel through his hand, just how nervous Ben was, clammy and a slight shake could be felt through his touch. With one deep breath in each, they both squeezed their eyes shut and stepped through the watery surface of the mirror.

Feeling as though all they had done was take a step forward, not feeling as though anything extreme had just happened, they both slowly opened their eyes.

It was dark and the air felt musty and heavy. Unlike the previous room, this one had a window, with the smallest amount of light coming in from the full moon outside. Although it wasn't much light, it did however reflect on some glass surfaces on the wall. Lined up on the opposite wall to the window, were photos, portraits of what seemed to be the patients from many years ago. All faded, some with cracks in the glass and some were in pieces scattered all over the floor behind an old wooden desk.

Upon the desk, an old, patterned glass vase, dust covering every rim and crease in the glass. Inside the vase were old, dried, what may have once resembled wilted flowers, covered in fluffy spider webs.

Abi walked towards the photos on the wall, past the old wooden desk, sliding her finger across the dusty surface, leaving clean lines amongst the filth on the desk.
As she drew closer to the portraits, she noticed a metal plaque above the remaining frames on the wall.

Brushing the dust off of the copper plaque with her sleeve, she revealed the wording.
Wall of successes.

"Are all these people, those that the hospital believed to have been cured?!" Abi exclaimed.

Ben had picked up a large book from the messy desk. Blew across the surface to remove the years of dirt that had collected on the open pages.

Names upon names were listed down the pages along with their conditions, treatments and their progress.

Name: Graham Holzer.
Age:28.
Condition: Arousal by the same sex.
Treatment: Electrotherapy
Cured: Yes

Name: Fiona Gordan
Age: 16
Condition: Insane, uncontrollable screaming towards men
Treatment: Hydrotherapy baths, Metrazol-convulsive therapy
Cured: Yes

"Oh my god! Poor kid!" Ben said in sorrow.
"Abi, I think you're right. This book contains the names of those believed to have been cured with the different so-called treatments. Look..." he said pointing at the entry for Fiona Gordon.
"This poor girl was forced to take Metrazol!"
"What did that do?" Abi questioned.
"It's a drug that caused you to have seizures and left the patients unconscious. They believed it would shock peoples brains out of mental health, leaving them to be normal again." He advised her.

"Seriously?! It makes me sick that people were forced into these methods of treatment!" she replied in a state of shock. "And that girl was only 16! What must have happened to her?! Look at her condition... screaming at men... something bad must have happened to her for her to end up reacting like that! And I bet the staff didn't even think about what would have caused her to act out like that.
It isn't treatment, it's bloody torture!"

Abi took the book and sat in an old wooden chair next to the desk. She continued to flick through the pages in search of Katrina.
Collete Simmons.
Justin Marvis.

Lenor Jacobs.
Name after name after name.
"What if we never get the truth Ben?" She asked hopelessly.
"We will Abi, don't give up."

And just as he replied to Abi, she turned to the next page and there she was.

Name: Katrina Taylor.
Age: 24
Condition: Delusions, hallucinations
Treatment: Hydrotherapies
Cured: Yes

"Here!" Abi announced.
"They really thought she was crazy didn't they?" She said sadly, placing the book on the desk.
Sliding the book onto the desk she accidentally knocked something heavy from the desk, sending it falling to the floor with a smash.
"Seriously?!" She exclaimed.

Ben brought his torchlight to the area they believed the object to fall.
The light reflected up into their eyes. Abi reached down to pick up the item.
She had an item in each hand.
She had knocked off a metal name plaque. It had fallen onto and smashed a framed photo that would have once been displayed on 'The Wall of The Cured'.
The name on the plaque was Margaret Davies.
"This is the head nurse's office." She explained after remembering the name.
"There must be more information on Katrina in here!"
She turned the frame over in her hand, a familiar face looked back at her. Katrina's 'cured' portrait.
"What happened, Katrina? Where did you go?" As the words left Abi's lips, the drawer of the desk fell onto her lap, as if a sign from Katrina.

Looking through the drawer, she came across a small wooden box. She lifted the lid. On the inside of the lid was stuck a note. Opening the note revealed wording stating it was the property of Katrina.
Looking back into the box and removing a piece of purple velvet, she discovered a piece of jewellery. A big black stone mounted in a metal casing on a silver chain. It was a Black obsidian necklace once belonging to Katrina.

"Safe." A whisper came from behind her. It was a comforting voice and made Abi feel calm. She placed the necklace around her neck, feeling as though Katrina wanted her to have it.

Ben pacing around the room, had missed what had happened entirely.
He looked around the room, shining his torch onto every surface. His light fell onto a stack of books with tatty covers and some without any covers at all.
He started searching through the books to see what he could find.
"Treatment books, records... hang on... Diary...."
Sure enough, as Ben opened up the book, there on the first page read, 'Diary of Margaret Davies'.

"Jackpot!" He exclaimed.
And as the words left his mouth the window smashed inwards sending shards of glass towards them. They both jumped to hide behind the desk to avoid getting slashed by the flying glass. Abi came out unscathed, however Ben was not so lucky. He was a little further away from the desk, whereas Abi was still sitting at the desk and just had to jump down.
As Ben threw himself through the air towards the desk, one single piece of glass plunged itself into the top of his arm. However, due to the adrenaline rushing through his body, it wasn't himself that realised what had happened.

"Ben! Your arm!" she shouted in a panic.
Looking down at his arm, he noticed the shard sticking out from his skin and the blood dripping down onto the diary still clutched in his hands.
He started to pull the piece of glass from his flesh and the whole room seemed to shake.
"Abi we need to get out of here!" Ben shouted.
"The window!" Abi replied.
Ben pulled an old bookcase underneath the small window and got Abi to climb out first.
She climbed up towards the window. Looking back down at Ben to make sure he was still there, she was surprised by what she saw.

There, standing behind Ben... Jack.

"Jack?!" She shouted down to Ben in confusion.
Ben turned around and Jack went for his throat.
"Ben!!" She screamed.
"Go Abi! Get out!" He screamed back at her as Jack tackled him to the floor.

Jack had Ben pinned to the floor, his hands around his throat but more than that... a dark shadow hovered over him as if controlling him like a puppet.

Abi being Abi, not about to leave him behind, jumped down from the bookcase.
"You can't have them!" She shouted at the darkness hovering above.
Ben passed out under the pressure of Jack's hands and at the sound of Abi's voice, the gloomy figure dropped Jack to the floor, releasing him from its control and knocking him out as his head hit the stone floor.
"Oh can't I.." The creature replied shallowly with its hoarse voice. "And what are you going to do to stop me?"
Nearing closer and closer to Abi, the shape of the creature shifted into that of the Nanny! Helen!
"What did you do to her?! What did you do to Katrina?!" Abi demanded strongly.
"You're about to find out!" Helen replied with a cackle.

Helen swarmed towards Abi. The moonlight then shone onto Abi's necklace, sending reflected light back towards Helen, putting her to a complete halt.
The light reflected at her caused a deafening screech to escape from inside her and she disappeared back into darkness.

Abi ran over to Ben and Jack.
A liquid that glistened in the moonlight that came in through the window, surrounded them.
Blood!
Shaking Ben as tears started to pool in her eyes, "Ben! Ben, please be alive! Please!" She begged. "Please! You can't leave me!" She demanded.
"Urghh." A shallow moan came from Ben and he lifted his hand to his throat shakily.
"Abi." he said coarsely. The attack to his throat left him unable to talk very clearly.
"Oh thank god you're okay!" she cried, leaning in to kiss him.
"But that means..." she stopped.
Looking over to Jack, she noticed he had not moved and there was a dark pool right by his head.
"Jack?" She questioned as she crawled over to him.
She took his hand and squeezed it.
Ben rose slowly and joined Abi. Kneeling beside Jack, Ben placed his fingers on Jack's neck to check his pulse.
"He's dead." He said in shock.

He pulled Abi in close and she cried in his arms.

A silent tear left his eye and dropped on top of Abi's auburn hair.

"We need to leave Abi. We need to get an ambulance here and without phone signal, we need to leave him and get help." He said calmly, trying to comfort her and at the same time, get some control of the situation.

"You're right. I wish we had never come. This is all my fault. I am so sorry Ben. I should have never brought you and Jack into this. It's all my fault he's dead." She cried.

"Don't think like that. Let's get out of here," he replied, helping her up.

They made their way back to the bookshelf to climb out of the moonlit window.

Abi climbed up and out into the open air. She jumped down onto the ground outside.

Ben reached the top of the bookcase and before going out of the window he looked back to where his friend lay dead.

"What?" He questioned.

His body was gone. But he was dead... wasn't he?

"Where's he gone? Jack?" He called out. But no reply.

Ben joined Abi outside.

"Jacks gone."

Abi walked up to him and gave him a gentle hug.

"I know. I'm so sorry. This should never have happened."

"NO! He's actually gone! I looked back down to him from the bookcase and his body wasn't there! There's no way he could have gotten out, even if he did survive. But it's not possible... I checked his pulse myself. There was NO pulse!" Ben replied in confusion.

"You don't think she.." Abi started.

"Took him? Yes, I think she has. Abi, we still need to get out of the grounds. The gate is locked and there are no holes in the fence, so that means we have to go back inside. We have to find the tunnels again.

"Which way do you think we should go?" Abi asked, thinking about how to get back into the Asylum... which is the last thing she wanted to do.

This investigation had already caused so much hurt and not to mention death. She couldn't care less about all of the equipment that they had left inside. She just wanted to get out and as far away from the building as possible. There had been so many near deaths for Ben and the thought of being without him wasn't worth thinking of.

Although they hadn't been together very long, they had been friends for years and so always had been a part of each other's lives and she couldn't imagine it any other way.

"Let's try this way," Ben replied, taking her hand and starting to walk in the direction of what seemed to be gardens.

There were pebbles beneath their feet. Weeds and long grasses smothered the stones they walked on.

There were broken stone planters on the ground which, back in their day, were probably beautifully planted with flowers.

It was hard to make out the way ahead of them as the fog appeared thicker and thicker as they continued.

They followed the remnants of the pebble path further until they noticed something ahead through the fog. Some sort of structure on the ground ahead, but due to the fog, they couldn't make it out clearly.

They continued their approach to discover a stone well. Weeds climbed up the old cracked stones covered in wet, green moss.

Abi stepped right up to it, placed her hands on the damp stones and looked in.

Chapter 21

"Thank you so much for believing in me. No one else here would have done this for me." Katrina said, thanking a lady for her help out of the asylum. "You have no idea how much this means to me."

"I'm just sorry I didn't realise sooner. You didn't deserve all of those sessions. This is the least I could do. Now leave before anyone realises what we have done." She urged Katrina.

Katrina brought her into a tight, thankful hug before turning her back on the Asylum that tortured her for so long.

"Oh, one more thing." Katrina said, placing her hand over her chest.

She pulled a necklace from under her clothing. A black obsidian necklace, a beautiful contrast against the pure white snow background.

"Here, I want you to have this. Get out as soon as you can, but in the meantime, use this necklace to keep yourself safe." She place the necklace over the nurses head, squeezed both of her hands and turned to make her way down the asylum steps.

The nurse walked back indoors from the snow-covered steps, leaving Katrina out in the cold on her own.

Katrina took a deep, frosty breath.

For the first time in ages, she finally felt hopeful and free. Opening her mouth, she released a warm cloud of breath and she started to make her way through the snow-covered gardens.

Each step gave a satisfying crunch beneath her as she walked through the untouched snow.

Feeling as free as a bird, she spun around in the snow, full of happiness and plunged herself into the snow laughing. She laid in the snow, her eyes closed, happy tears rolled down her cheeks as she made snow angels and imagined having her son with her to play in the snow.

"Having fun, are we?" A woman's voice came from behind her.
Katrina opened her eyes to find Helen standing over her with an angry expression across her face.
"Not on my watch!" She grabbed Katrina by her hair, dragging her through the snow. Katrina kicked and screamed but no one could hear her.
"You really thought you'd get away did you?! and I know just who helped you as well! Neither of you will ruin this for me!" Helen slammed Katrina's body into the side of an icy stone well in the centre of the gardens.
The trees surrounded the area in a circle making them invisible to anyone from the asylum.
"No one will ever know where you are, they will never find you and will never come looking for you!" She growled, grabbing Katrina's head and smashing it into the stone, over and over.

Blood dripped down from her brow, into the glistening snow.

"No one will ever get in the way of James and I!" Helen whispered malevolently.
She bent down and dragged Katrina's lifeless body up the side of the well and pushed her inside, her body plummeting into the bottomless darkness.

Helen grabbed some branches from the trees surrounding the well and brushed over all of the drag marks and footprints to cover up the atrocious murder she had just committed.
Scooping up the blood-stained snow from the floor, she threw it down into the well to be with Katrina's body.
Believing she had covered up her actions, she made her way to the doorsteps of the asylum.

She pushed open the doors violently, letting in a huge gust of wind and snow.
The nurse behind the reception desk rushed over to her.

"Welcome back Ms Watson." The nurse greeted as she brushed the snow from Helen's shoulders.
"Thank you" She replied stonily.

143

"Oh Ms Watson, are you bleeding? I can see to that for you!" She insisted.
"No, no, just a scratch! I slipped on the icy steps as I approached." She lied as she pulled her coat sleeve down to cover her blood-soaked shirt sleeve.
"Are you sure? I have some bandages behind my desk." She asked sincerely.
"Just leave it!" Helen demanded. "Now where is Dr Watson?"
The nurse was taken aback in shock after offering to help Helen.
"Uh, uh.. I'll let him know you're here." She stumbled.
"Don't bother! In his office is he?" Helen didn't even wait for the nurse to answer her and headed straight for Arthurs office.

"Hello cousin." She said, bursting through the office doors and quickly slamming them shut behind her.
Arthur jumped at the sound and dropped his pen on top of his paperwork.
"Helen, what are you doing here?"
"She's dead!" She announced happily, a big, evil grin growing across her face.
"Who's dead?" Arthur questioned.
"Who do you think, idiot?! Katrina!"
"Wait what? She was just released?" He questioned.
"I know." She replied.
"Helen, what have you done?" He said, rubbing his head in frustration.
"Does it matter?! She's gone! Out of the way! I can finally have James all to myself. I will no longer be a maid, but a doting wife and mother!" she said, full of excitement.
"Are you bloody crazy?!" He whispered angrily, hurrying to the door to make sure no one could have overheard.
"Careful Arthur!" She said angrily, "I'm not the only one with secrets, remember!"
"What if someone finds out, Helen? Then what?" He asked.
"No-one will ever find out, not unless you tell them. She's hidden and I've covered my tracks well."
"Where is she?"
"I think it's best that I kept that to myself Arthur." She replied. "If I'm the only one who knows then no one will ever find her."
"Does James know?" He asked.
"Of course not! He can never know. This is where you come into the plan."
"I don't want any part of this Helen."
"Tough. If you want your secret to remain a secret, then you will help with mine!" She demanded.
"What do you need me to do?" He sighed.
"Inform James of her escape. That she did in fact run off with that man who worked here. Contact the press as well to keep an eye out for an insane lady who requires immediate hospital care."

"This is the last thing I do Helen. I will not keep playing these games for you. This is it. Over." He said. "You leave here and never come back."

"That's fine by me. What do I need you for when I will have the life I always wished for with James?" She laughed. "Deal."

They shook hands and she turned to leave.

"Oh and one last thing. Your head nurse will no longer be working here. I spoke to her on her way out and thought you should know she has already left." She lied.

She left his office and closed the door behind her, but she had one last stop before she left.

Luckily, another patient had the attention of the nurse on reception, so she passed by without being noticed and headed to Nurse Davies office.

"I've got you Abi! Don't let go!" Ben cried out.

Abi was dangling on the inside of the well. Realising that her vision had triggered her to fall straight over the top, she let out a scream.

"Don't let me fall Ben!" she cried. "My necklace! It's caught."

Indeed, her necklace was caught on the stone inside the well, so every time Ben tried to pull her back up, the chain would pull on her neck.

She slowly tugged one hand out of Ben's.

"No Abi! Hold on, it's too dangerous! It's just a necklace!"

"I can't lose it! It's Katrina's necklace. She said it would protect me!" She begged.

She carefully pulled the necklace free from the icy stone and reached back up to Ben.

"Quick! Pull me up!" She shouted up to him.

She placed her feet onto the stone wall inside the well and tried to push up as Ben pulled.

Her footing slipped, sending her face-first into the wall and nearly losing Ben's grip. Ben's grip tightened.

"I've got you! Are you okay?!" He called out.

All he could hear was Abi's cries echoing down into the depth of the well.

His grip tightened, his face tensed and he slowly edged Abi out of the darkness and onto the damp ground surrounding the stony death trap.

Ben dropped to the ground pulling her close and checked her head to make sure she was okay.

145

"Just a scratch." He confirmed, kissing the graze on her head.

"Why did you do that Abi?"

"Do what?" She asked, her brow pressed together.

"You went into the well Abi! You screamed out as if someone was after you and head first into the well!" He explained. "Don't you not remember? How hard did you hit your head Abi?"

"No... it wasn't me. It was Katrina. She's down there. Helen smashed her head against the well and threw her in there."

"What?! you had another vision?! but this happened in a matter of seconds Abi."

"I don't know how it works but it happened Ben. Someone was helping Katrina to leave and just as she thought she was free, Helen found her and killed her before she could go home." She explained.

"Oh, poor Katrina. Who was helping her?"

"I never saw her face, but I know it was a woman. Helen got her cousin to cover up the murder, so even James didn't know she was dead. He thought she had escaped and ran off with Thomas."

"So no-one ever knew she was dead?" He asked in amazement.

"No. The whole world just carried on without her." She said clutching at her necklace.

"Wait... the necklace... In my vision, Katrina gave this necklace to the person who helped her. We found the necklace in Nurse Davies office! She got Katrina out, she must have!" Katrina exclaimed.

Ben dropped his bag from his back, onto the floor and reached for the diary he had found back in the room where they had just left Jack.

He flicked through the pages to her last few entries.

Ben read it out loud to Abi.

"Today Katrina finally left our so called care. I wish I hadn't had been so brainwashed in this business. Today I will be handing in my notice. They will never know why but I will further down the line, when it is safe to do so, reveal them for who they really are. The doctors will not get away with what they have done here.

Katrina gave me her necklace as a gift of thanks and she also believes it will help to protect me, whilst I attempt to expose the Asylum. I only wish I had opened my eyes a lot sooner. So many lives could have been saved.

I feel guilty, disgusting and highly responsible for a lot of what has happened in this place.

I wish Katrina well and hope her family life can improve." Ben finished.

"She did help Katrina." Abi sighed.

"That was her final entry. Why wouldn't she take this with her? Why leave it at the Asylum, especially as she was wanting to expose them?" Ben questioned.
"Helen... Helen not only wanted Katrina out of the way, somehow she knew Nurse Davies had helped her and she wanted them both dead. Just before my vision ended, she went after her ad I can only imagine what she did to her." Abi explained.

They heard a metallic click in the distance and an eerie noise as if a door was opening.
They both stood and started walking in the direction of the sound, working their way through the now thinning fog.

"The gate!" Abi cried in disbelief. "It's open!"
"Find James and tell him the truth." A calm voice came from behind them.
They both spun around to find Katrina standing behind them.
"Katrina!" Abi gasped.
"Thank you for finding the truth, there is yet more to discover. But all will be revealed once you have spoken to James." Katrina informed them with a hushed voice.
"James? But where can we find him." Ben asked, still not believing his eyes.
"Go home," Katrina said, her voice fading.
"But..." Abi started.
"Go home."
And right before them, she evaporated into the cold, icy air.

"Did that really just happen?" Ben asked in amazement. "Like.. that ACTUALLY happened... I didn't imagine that, did I?" He questioned shakily.
"That actually happened," Abi responded... "THAT ACTUALLY HAPPENED!" She exclaimed happily. "We actually helped Katrina. We learned the truth about her! We know who killed her."
"Yes, but she also said there is more to learn, remember? We need to find James."
"The house... My house!" She said as a memory came flooding back to her.
"He's at my house! Remember the time I had someone come to fit my kitchen.. and the man disappeared... That was James. "
"We need to get home! But how? The car is useless and our phones have no signal."
Ben gestured at his phone, taking it out of his pocket to remind her.
But there upon the screen... two bars of signal.
"I have signal!" he said in excitement. "We can get out of here!"

The sun had barely started appearing on the horizon. The sun's rays beamed through the fog and glistened on the icy surfaces and dew on the ground.

"I don't think any taxi services are going to be open just yet Ben." She sighed, looking at how beautiful the world was now looking with a hint of sunshine. You could almost forget all the torture and nightmares this place had caused... almost.

"We can start walking to the next town. By then we should be able to get some help and get home." Ben planned.

"Jack!" Abi remembered. "We need to get help for Jack. We can't leave him here. His family needs to know what happened."

Ben's face dropped.

Through all the terrifying moments that had just played out with Abi, Jack had slipped his mind. Guilt flooded him and tears started to pool in his eyes.

"Nope, I need to be strong for Abi." He thought to himself, taking a deep breath. He took out his phone and called for an ambulance.

"Ambulance please." He said, holding the phone to his ear.

"My friend is dead. We're at Blue Waters Asylum."

It took about 30 minutes for the police and an ambulance to arrive.

"Can you tell us what happened?" A policeman asked. He was tall, with dark hair and deep brown eyes. He had his notepad and pen ready to take notes.

"Jack is a paranormal investigator. We decided to join him and come down here for the night to see if the location was haunted. We ended up in a room, I fell through the unstable wall which is how we found the room. It had no doors and just a window. It was as if he had gone mad, he lunged at me strangling me until I passed out. I woke up and he was dead on the floor next to me." Ben told the officer.

"And where were you when this happened?" He asked Abi.

Ben squeezed her hand.

"I was hiding behind a desk in the same room. I was frightened. Jack had already gone for me earlier in the night."

"I made her hide as I was scared of what he would do to her. It was unlike him to act like this." Ben added in Abi's defence.

"So you say you woke up to him next to you dead... so where is he now?" The officer asked.

"We don't know. I made Abi climb out of the room first and when it was my turn, before I headed out of the window, I looked back down and he had vanished." Ben replied.

"But you said there were no doors?" Questioned the officer.

"He could have got out through the crumbled wall though, but I checked his pulse. He was dead. I know it sounds ridiculous, but that's what happened. I can't explain it." Ben replied.

"And there was no-one else with you. It was just you two and Jack?"

"Yes, just the three of us," Abi confirmed.

They left out all the stuff about the visions and the murders. The police wouldn't believe them anyway.

"Okay, I'll get my men to search the building for your friend. In the meantime, officer Bryant will escort you home. I'll require you not to take any upcoming trips in case we have more questions, understood?" The officer states.

"Yes, of course." They both reply.

"We will find your friend." He assured them.

Chapter 22

The sun had now risen as the police car approached and pulled up outside of Abi's home. The morning sun fell onto the house, giving it an appearance of having a warm, inviting glow.

"Thank you for bringing us home," Abi said to the officer as she rubbed Ben's leg.

Ben, exhausted from the night's turn of events, had fallen asleep on the journey home and awoke when Abi rubbed his leg.

"Huh? Oh, sorry. Thank you officer and do please contact us if you need any more information."

The officer nodded at them as they stepped out of the car.

Ben put his arm around Abi as the officer drove off and started walking towards the house.

"Abi, shall we go to mine instead. We could both do with some rest and I doubt we'd get any at yours." He suggested.

"Good idea. I'm exhausted. James has been here for years, a few hours won't hurt." She agreed.

Hand in hand, they walked away from the steps to Abi's home and down the path to Ben's.

"I'm so glad we're neighbours," She admitted as they approached his front door.

Relief overcame the both of them as they stepped into his house.
Sunlight filled the rooms before them. The complete opposite to the building in which they had just come from.

The Asylum was dark, dingy and a complete mess, with spider webs hanging from the ceilings, paint chipping off of the walls and dust-filled carpets.

Ben's home was clean, modern and bright, with citrus filled air where the home was clearly cleaned every day. Not a cobweb in sight and not one dusty surface.

"Oh it's good to be home." Ben sighed, pulling Abi in for a hug.
"Why don't I go run you a nice warm bubble bath?" He offered, kissing Abi's forehead.
"That sounds amazing." She replied, kissing his lips in return.

Ben made his way up to the bathroom and started running a bath for her.
Meanwhile, Abi walked into the living area and sat on the black leather sofa.
Wrapping the contrasting white blanket around her, she curled up and before she knew it, she was asleep.

Ben left the tub to fill and walked back downstairs to find Abi asleep on the sofa.
He pushed a curl of fiery hair away from her face and behind her ear, taking in how at peace she looks.
He left her to rest on the sofa and went into the kitchen to find some food.

Looking in the fridge he found some strawberries and grapes and decided that pancakes were this morning's breakfast option.
Pancakes with Lemon and sugar, with a side of fruit.
Grabbing the ingredients from the cupboard and a frying pan from the shelf above the stove, he started making up some pancakes for the two of them.

He slid two pancake rolls and a handful of fruit onto two plates and strolled into the front room. He placed them on the coffee table before heading back to grab two glasses of apple juice.

The smell of the freshly made pancakes was enough to make Abi's tummy growl so loud that it woke her up.

"Nice nap?" Ben asked as he handed her a plate of food.
151

"For once, amazing. I don't care how long or short it was. It was just nice to not dream or have any nightmares." She replied, rubbing her eyes with one hand and the other hand taking the plate.

"The bath!" Jack panicked, completely forgetting he had left the bathtub filling for Abi.

He almost dropped his plate before setting it back down and running as fast as he could to the bathroom.

Bubbles had just started to float over the side of the bath onto the floor, being soaked up by the black Egyptian cotton bath mat.

Grabbing a towel from the heated rail, he starts mopping up the soapy bubbles from the floor that evaded the bath mat.

"Fancy some breakfast?" Abi asked, standing behind him with his plate of pancakes and fruit.

"No." He said with a smile.

He removed Abi's clothes layer by layer and helped her into the bath, before removing his own clothes and joining her.

The bubbles overflowed once more as they both stepped into the ivory white tub surrounded by soft, glowing candles.

He climbed in behind Abi, took a sponge and started rubbing down her back and shoulders, the warm soapy water trickling over her shoulders and back into the tub.

Knock, knock, knock.

"Oh you have got to be kidding," Ben said with frustration.
"It's okay, find out who it is and come back," Abi said, her hand squeezing his.

Ben climbed out of the bath, water dripping onto the already wet floor. He wrapped a soft, black towel around his waist and headed downstairs. He opened the front door, but there was no one there. In place of what he thought would be a person at the door, instead sat a letter on the doormat.

He picked it up and shut the door. He walked slowly back into the lounge, he opened the envelope and pulled out a folded piece of paper. He unfolds it to discover one word. One name. James.

"Can't you give us just one day?" He sighed out loud. Knowing what he had to do, he walked back up the stairs and into the bathroom.

"We need to go to yours." Ben informed Abi as he walked back in. He handed the piece of paper to Abi that had just arrived on his doorstep.

"James." She sighed. "Okay." she said reluctantly. "Maybe he couldn't wait a few more hours."

Ben held out his hand to Abi and helped her out of the bath. They both made their way to his bedroom and got changed. Abi changed into a super comfy lounge set. As her comfort day was taken away from her, she at least wanted to feel comfortable today.

Ben threw on a pair of denim jeans and a tight, fitted black shirt.

"Seriously?" She said looking at him, lust filling her entire body.
"What?" He asked, looking down at his outfit.

"Why do you have to look so good, when I'm standing here in comfy clothes, looking less than attractive right now." She said, walking up to him and running her fingers slowly through his hair.
Ben placed his hands on either side of her waist.
"You're beautiful no matter what you wear." He replied, kissing her on her lips.
"Now let's go find James so we can get this all over with and I can finally have you to myself." He smiled.
"Let's go." She smiled softly in return.

They make their way back down the stone stairs and out the front door, into the sunshine.

"Luna!" Abi called out sadly.

There before them stood Luna. Her eyes were bloodshot and puffy. She fell to her knees in front of them without saying a word. Sobs bellowed from within her.

"Oh Luna." Abi ran over to Luna who was kneeling on the pathway to the house. Her world had been torn apart from the loss of Jack.
"I'm so sorry Luna. I should never have got either of you involved. I wish there was something I could do."
"The police came to question me about Jack." Trying to get her words out through her tears. "They can't find him. They actually told me to expect the worst! Saying

there is no sign of him but there were traces of his blood throughout the building."

And with those last words, Luna broke down even further.
She clutched her fingers in her hair, her grip getting tighter and her face even more scrunched up as she wailed.

"What happened to him?! I need Jack!"
Abi held onto Luna so tight. She looked up at Ben and mouthed to him, "What do I do?"
He ran a hand through his hair as he thought.
"We will find him, Luna. If the police don't, then we WILL." He promised her.

He placed a hand on her shoulder and helped her up. He embraced her in a comforting hug.
"Trust me. We will not let him stay missing. We will find him. We need to stay strong, okay? Come with me. Let's go to Abi's and get a cup of tea."

Luna agreed, took his hand and the three of them walked towards Abi's.

They came to a stop on Abi's doorstep.
"Luna, before we go in, you should know... we found out the truth about Katrina but for all of this to come to an end, James needs to know. I know that this is a really crap time to say the least, but I'm hoping that once James knows, everything else will come to the surface, we will find Jack and all of this will be over."
"I understand," Luna replied, tears still flowing from her stinging eyes.
Abi hugged her once more. "We will get through this Luna."

Abi turned to the door, placed her key in the lock and turned until she heard a click.
She took a deep breath and turned the handle. She slowly pushed the door open and stepped inside her home.
Looking around, everything was just as they had left it. The whole house sat in silence.
Seeing that it appeared safe to go in, she invited Ben and Luna in.

Luna and Ben went and sat at the dining table whilst Abi went into the kitchen to make some tea.

After all the nightmares they had all been through, she opted for a tea blend that would calm their senses. She placed a couple of rosebuds and some dried lavender into the strainer inside of her glass teapot and poured hot water in.
The colour from the roses started to leak out into the water, making it a pretty, pink hue.
The smell of lavender could be smelt on the steam released from the teapot spout.
She grabbed 3 teacups and poured the stress relief mixture into the mugs and took them through to Ben and Luna.
She also placed a pot of honey on the table before them and added one teaspoon to her own cup.

"Here guys, drink up. This should help. It's a lavender and rose blend to help with stress. It should help with calming."
"My nan used to make this tea all the time. How do you know about tea blends?" Luna asked, bringing the tea up to her nose so she could smell it. A memory flooded her mind, sitting with her nan in front of the fireplace, wrapped up in a blanket, her grandmother reading her favourite book to her.

"I'm not really sure. I've always been interested in herbs and their medicinal properties." Abi replied.
"You have crystals in your home, a knowledge of herbs and you have visions. Abi, have you ever thought that maybe you're a witch?" Luna asked.

"A witch?" Abi laughed. "I'm not magic."
"No, not Hollywood magic... you do things with intent. You do things to help others. You like being in nature. So many people misjudge what a witch is. Don't think 'Harry Potter'. Think more... hippy, I suppose. We all have different gifts. You're intuitive, maybe even a healer with the way you use herbs."
"Really? I mean... I suppose it would make sense." Abi took a sip of her steamy tea.
"Ahh!" She called out as the hot liquid burnt her tongue and spilt onto her top.

She almost dropped the mug onto the table as she ran to get a towel to dry up the hot tea.
"I'm going to have to change." Abi sighed.
"There's some cakes in the fridge if you want to help yourselves. I'll be back down in a minute." She said as she headed to the stairs.

She stopped at the bottom and looked up. Knowing she would be going on her own set the hairs on her arms on edge.
"Just breathe." She whispered to herself and started making her way up the stairs.
155

She started walking along the hallway towards her bedroom and heard a creek behind her.

She stopped dead in her tracks. Her ears were now on high alert. She thought she heard a shuffle from the room behind her. She turned on the spot and headed to the room from where she heard the noise and pushed the door open gently.

Moonlight filled the room to reveal a nursery.

"Where is he, Helen? " James asked.
"Who?" Helen replied as she put away Henry's Jacket.
"Henry. On my way home I was stopped by an elderly woman who admitted to seeing you the day that Henry went missing. She said you had his pram with you and you were meeting another couple." He explained.
"I didn't go to the park that day James. She's probably losing her mind and saw someone else with a buggy." She replied.
"She saw you leave the house Helen"
"Stupid old bat!"
"Excuse me?" James questioned.
"Why can't people keep their noses out of other people's business," Helen said, as she put her hand around the handle of a knife from her pocket.
"What did you do?!" He exclaimed desperately.
"We could have been so good together you and I. Start our own family. He's better off with them anyway." She said ignoring his question entirely.

Her hand gripped the knife tighter and she spun around. She lunged at James aiming the knife right at his chest.
He grabbed her arm, stopping her from plunging the knife into his flesh.

"Helen, what are you doing?! Why are you doing this?! You're acting crazy!" He shouted as he twisted her arm around her back.
"Don't call me CRAZY!" She screamed into his ear.

The high pitched screech made him release his grip on her arm and she spun around scratching his arm with her knife.
Blood started to show through his white shirt.
She threw herself at him once more and as she struck him, he pushed her away defending himself from another blow.
She stumbled backwards, shattering the window behind her and sending her plummeting to the ground.

"Helen!" He called out as he leant out the window.

There she lay in a twisted mess on the garden patio. Full of panic, he paced the nursery. He had lost his wife, his son and now his so-called 'friend'.

"What is happening!" Both hands on his head as he walked from the door to the window and back again.
He started feeling hot and sweaty and he ran to the bathroom as quickly as he could. The stress and the sudden death of Helen had made him sick to his stomach.
He cleaned himself up, splashing water on his face and leaning over the basin for a moment to collect his thoughts.

"It's just an accident. You didn't cause this." He told himself. "Why do I keep losing everyone... oh god what will people think if I report her missing too!"

He hurried to the front of the house and looked outside. By sheer coincidence a horse and carriage were sitting out front and the driver stood by it smoking a cigarette.

He cleared his throat, "Excuse me young man, are you waiting on anyone?" James asked.
"No sir, just on a break." He replied.
"Would you mind just waiting there a moment? I require your service." James asked.
"Of course sir." The young man replied.

James walked away from the window and snuck outside behind the carriage. He stepped slowly towards the man just finishing his cigarette with his back towards him. Swiftly, he grabbed his head and twisted as fast as he could, snapping his delicate neck.
"I'm sorry. I didn't want this to happen." James apologised as he dragged the driver into the carriage.
He ran into the garden and picked up Helens now stone heavy body. He carried her through the darkness and into the carriage, placing her next to the man he had just killed and closed the door on them.
He climbed up onto the carriage, took the stirrups in his hands and with one swift action, got the horses trotting in the direction of the river.

He navigated the dark streets until he finally reached the river at the bottom of a steep hill. He pulled to one side and jumped down from his perch.

He searched around the edge of the river for heavy rocks to place into their pockets.

And he's in luck.

He pulled the bodies down to the riverside, added rocks into the pockets of his victims and tied a big one around each of their waists, in hopes that the bodies would never be found floating on the surface.

After finishing the knot on Helen's waist, he pulled them one at a time into the deepest part of the river and let them sink heavily to the bottom.

He walked out, dripping wet and cold and sat on the river bank and waited a while to make sure the bodies didn't surface.

He sat there shivering and as the realisation set in of what had just happened, grief struck his body. Tears flowed from his eyes, down his cheeks and onto his already water-soaked clothes.

"God please forgive me, please dear God." He repeated over and over.

The night grew colder and the longer he stayed the more his body would shake.

"I need to get home." He said out loud to himself.

He walked back to the carriage. Instead of taking the carriage home, he untied the horses and let them run free, leaving the carriage idle by the riverside on the bridge, as if abandoned. He loosened the nut on one of the back wheels and popped it in his pocket. He pulled the wooden wheel from the carriage and propped it up beside it.

He then started making his way back home by foot, discarding the bolt in one of the hedgerows on the way.

Upon his return home, he got to thinking of a way to explain Helen's disappearance.

A note!

My Dear James,
Please do not come looking for me.
You will not find me.

Your son is safe.
My biggest wish was to have a beautiful loving family with you.
The loss of our little Henry is too much for me to bare, along with the depression that I see on your face every day.
My mind is all over the place, I don't know what to think anymore. Maybe I need help.
One minute I believe we can be a happy family and the next I want the whole world to be a black void.

I'm sorry.

Your dearest Helen.

"In the morning I will report her missing." He thought to himself. "Make her seem so love-struck and lost, maybe even the hospital will be in contact.

The next morning comes and he informs the police, the media and the hospital to be on the lookout for Helen, a lovestruck lady suffering mental illness.

As he returned home that evening, he noticed all the lights in the house were on.
He walked through the front door and the fireplace in the living room was ablaze, sending warmth into the entire house.
He closed the door softly behind him in an attempt to be as silent as possible, in case someone was waiting for him in the house.
He removed his shoes and stepped gently across the hallway, passing each room and taking a look into each before heading to the stairs.
He took one step at a time as carefully as he possibly could, his hand sliding up the wooden rail as he went further up the stairs.
He reached the top and final step with a loud creak below his foot.

"Damn it." He whispered to himself.
All of his hairs stood on end, as each candle lighting the home went out, leaving him in a mass of darkness.

"Jameeessssss." A low long whisper called out behind him.
"No. No, it can't be." He tried to convince himself, but he knew this voice far too well.
"Thought you could get rid of me did you?" The female voice became angrier with every word.
James turned around slowly and there, floating up the stairs towards him, was the

familiar face of a woman whom he had just discarded.

"Helen?!" He exclaimed nervously. "No, no. You're not here. You're in the river!"

"Well that's where you left my body to rot didn't you James?!" She accused. "And now you're going to pay!"

Helen's spirit flew right through him sending him stumbling to the floor, unable to grab the handrail quick enough, he went tumbling down the stairs and when he finally reached the last step, his head whacked against the wall breaking his neck and splitting his head open.

"Abi has been a while." Ben said with worry.

"I'm going to check on her. Will you be okay for a few moments?" He asked Luna.

"Yeah, I'm fine." Luna replied as she headed to the sofa to lay down for a moment. "A little light-headed but I'm fine."

"I'll grab you a glass of water, one sec."

James walked into the kitchen and grabbed a glass from the drying rack and filled it with fresh water. On the way back into the living room, he grabbed a blanket and placed it over Luna and handed her the water.

"Thank you Ben." She said calmly before taking a sip and placing it on the table next to her.

"No worries. Why don't you take a nap? We will be back down in a bit." Ben suggested as he started walking towards the stairs.

He stood on the first few steps and called up.

"Abi? Are you okay?"

No reply.

He continued up the stairs and saw the spare room door open. He pushed the door fully open and found Abi on the floor by the window.

"Oh Abi! Not again!" He called out.

He bent down and held her head on his lap and stroked her forehead.

"Abi?" He said gently, as he ran his fingers through her hair.

"Abi, wake up." He says.

Abi starts to stir and rubs her head.

"She killed James." She said lowly.

"Well, James killed her, then she killed him." She said feeling very confused.

"Okay.. that doesn't make sense Abi. Take your time and start from the beginning." He replied softly.

"James worked out that Helen had given Henry away, in hopes of having James all to herself and starting a new family together. When he questioned her she went... crazy. She attacked him with a knife she had hidden in her pocket, but James pushed her away in defence. She went flying through the window and died on the garden patio." She confirmed to him.

"Oh James.." She sighed. "He killed someone else on purpose so he could get rid of Helen's body. He killed a man so that he could steal his carriage and get rid of Helen's body... in... in MY place! The river! It's my stream!" She exclaimed. "All those times I went to the stream, it used to be a river. James got rid of the bodies there!"

"So if he got rid of her body, then how did she kill him?" Ben asked.

"When he got home the following day, it looked as though someone was there. The fireplace was lit and candles were lit in every room. Her spirit was there. Her spirit attacked him as she did with us back at the Asylum. She sent him flying down the stairs, breaking his neck. He died here."

"Poor bloke." Ben sighed. "He lost his wife, his baby, not knowing what happened to either of them and then he died too!"

"Where's Luna? Maybe we could use her help to connect to James." Abi suggested.

"Like a seance?" Ben asked.

"Yeah. What do you think?" She replied.

"I mean, we've come this far, why not?" He confirmed. "Just have to see if Luna would be okay with that after everything that's happened."

"I know." Abi sighed sadly. "I just don't know what else to do."

Ben helped Abi up and walked her into her bedroom.

"Comfy clothes?" Ben asked as he opened her wardrobe.

"Please," She replied. "There should be a pink long sleeve top."

"Here." He said passing it to her, so she could change out of her wet clothes.

While she got changed, he tapped away on his phone.

The disappearance of Henry Taylor.

Articles upon articles pop up on his phone.

Baby goes missing.

Henry Taylor kidnapped?

Who has seen Henry Taylor?

2 years on from the disappearance of baby Henry Taylor

And finally...

Henry Taylor found after 4 years!

After the loss of his wife (Elizabeth Greenway), Mr John Greenway comes forward with, now 5 year old, Henry Taylor, who they had renamed Philip Greenway.

According to Mr Greenway, He and his wife had been trying for many years to have a baby, when a young woman answered their advertisements asking for help adopting a child. They met one day in the local park, just down the road from the Taylors home whilst Mr Taylor was at work.

Mr Taylor was subject to a miss-fortunate accident within his home, shortly after the disappearance of Ms Helen Watkins (The Nanny who kidnapped Henry and gave him away). As a result of his death, he never found out what happened to his son and now his son will never know his blood father or mother.

"So what happened to Henry?" Ben asked out loud.
"Huh?" Abi questioned.
"Oh, sorry. So I just found an article on the death of James and the fact that Henry would never know his true birth parents. The people who took him did come forward years after he was reported missing... well.. the man did. A couple took him but the woman passed away and that's why he then came forward. He probably felt like her death was a punishment for taking little Henry." Ben explained. "But it doesn't tell us what actually happened to Henry."
"Oh that poor kid, there must be some sort of information on him somewhere. I bet there is in the library. They must have some records on him." She wondered.
"We can add it to our list of to-dos." Ben added as Abi pulled her top down over her waist.
"Right, let's get back to Luna. I really don't want to ask her about doing a seance but I don't know how else to go forward." She revealed.

"I know. All we can do is ask." He said as he clutched her hand.

They made their way back down the stairs and into the living room but Luna was nowhere to be seen.

Abi's stomach now felt like it was in her throat and she started to panic.
"Luna?" She called out.
Abi walked around and out into the garden whilst Ben checked in the kitchen.
Failing those areas, they both made their way back up the stairs, checking each room along the hallway.
Still nowhere to be seen and only one place left to search.

The library!

Abi opened the door to the spiral staircase and called up. "Luna, are you up there?"
Nothing but silence travelled down the stairs.
They started to climb the dizzying stairs when halfway up, they had a cold breeze hit them.

They stopped in their tracks.

"Ben, something's not right." She said nervously.
"We need to see if she's up there Abi. If something is wrong, we need to make sure she is okay."
They continued carefully to the top of the stairs and the door to the library was already open.

Chapter 23

THUD.

Abi and Ben ran into the library and found Luna's body unconscious on the floor, but they weren't the only ones there.
There in front of Luna's body was what appeared to be Jack.

"Jack?!" Ben exclaimed.
"What? How?" He asked, stuck in confusion.

What stood before them, although he looked as alive as both Abi and Ben, was not a person with a beating heart.

"But we thought you were..." Abi started.
"Dead.. yep!" Jack interrupted.
"Jack I'm so sorry I didn't mean to." Ben started apologising, thinking Jack was back for revenge, just like Helen was for James.
"Ben, it's okay. Helen got to me. I was long gone before you left me in that room. You did what you had to do, both of you." He explained kindly.
"She flew straight through me, knocking me to the ground and I hit my head. Apparently, I like doing that." He said, trying to make light of the situation.
"With me being unconscious, she forced herself into my body and I didn't have the strength to fight her, so I was stuck outside of my body not able to get back in. By the time she left my body after messing with you two, it was too late. My heart

had stopped beating for so long, that my body was dead and I couldn't re-enter.
She just kept using my body as a tool to get at you both."
"Oh Jack." Abi sighed.

She walked towards him to hug him, obviously forgetting he was no longer alive.
Abi stumbled straight through him, falling to the floor. Jack looked down at her
and started laughing innocently.
Ben smiled and headed over to help her up.

"I forgot." She smiled at Jack as Ben helped her up.
"I wish we could have helped you, Jack." She said feeling helpless.
"I know, but there's nothing you could have done. Please don't feel bad." Jack
replied.

Luna started to stir.

"Guys. I could have sworn..." She started, as she rubbed her eyes."Jack!" She
gasped. "I wasn't seeing things!"
Tears started pooling in her eyes.
"Jack, what happened?" Luna asked tearfully. She reached out for his hand.
"Don't," Jack said, noticing her hand going for his, but it was too late. "I'm sorry
Luna. I wish I could feel you. I wish I could hold you." Jack said, holding back his
own tears.
"I can't do this Jack, not without you." She cried.
"You can honey, you must."
"Jack... I'm pregnant." She revealed, her hands holding onto her belly.

Abi walked over and embraced her as tears ran down her cheeks.
The tears Jack had just been holding back, had now been released. He would have
been a dad. He had never really thought of himself as a dad. He was just Jack.
Thrill seeker, ghost hunter, fun lover... but Dad?

As he thought about the possibility of having a child and having that child with
Luna, in this moment, what he wanted more than anything was to be alive again,
to be a dad and to be a husband to Luna.
The more he thought about it, the angrier he became.
The air around them started to cause a breeze to flow, but that breeze became
stronger and stronger. Books started to fly off their shelves.

It was Jack.

He had gotten so angry that he was causing poltergeist activity.

"Jack!" Luna called, knowing exactly where the blast of energy was coming from. At the sound of her voice, he snapped out of it.
"Was that me?!" He questioned in astonishment, as the last book fell to the ground. "Yes, baby," Luna replied.
"Sorry. That's new. It took a while for me to appear here. It took hours for me to work out how to travel from place to place. That was the first thing I tried to work out so I could appear to you all and let you know it wasn't your fault."
"So it wasn't Abi and Ben's fault?" Luna asked.
"No. I told them earlier whilst you were unconscious that it was Helen. She knocked me out, forced my soul from my body and I couldn't re-enter it as my body had already stopped functioning. It's Helen's fault I'm dead. It's Helen's fault I will never be a dad. She has taken everything from me."

"I know we can't do anything to bring you back Jack, and I so wish there was, but what if there was something to finally put a stop to her tormenting anyone else?" Abi suggested.
"How?" Jack replied, anger still on the edge of his voice.
"We need to find James's spirit. Let him know that his wife didn't just disappear on him." Ben replied.
"You found out what happened to Katrina?" Jack asked."Well, at least it wasn't all for nothing I suppose."
"Yes. Helen." Abi replied. "Helen killed her on the day of her release. She was finally free but Helen took her freedom away from her, she killed Katrina and her body now lies at the bottom of a well on the grounds of the asylum."
"You're telling me, she is still stuck in that hell hole?" Jack said, horrified at the thought of his own body being stuck in the dankness of the old asylum.
"Well, at least her body is. I'm not sure about her spirit. She obviously comes to me in my visions and mirrors, but I'm not sure as to what her capability is to be able to travel." Abi replied.
"So how do we contact this James then?" Jack asked.
"Through me." Luna said bluntly. "You need me to gain contact with him don't you?"
"Luna, I understand if you don't want to help us, especially in your condition now as well, but with your help we could contact James and safely, well, at least more safely with you than without you." Abi replied softly.
"I'll do it. I want that bitches soul to burn in hell for eternity." She said, her voice full of fury.

"We need a few supplies before we start" Luna instructed before going on to list what she needs. "Chalk, a black candle, a bowl of water, incense and Abi, one of your crystals. I will draw a pentagram on the ground and the other items will represent each element with each point of the pentagram representing; earth, fire, water and air, the last element is spirit."

"On it!" Abi exclaimed, as she rushed back down the stairs from the library, to her bedroom and grabbed a hand full of crystals that were lining her shelf, not knowing which crystal would be best. She then went to her dresser and tore open the drawer, where she had packs upon packs of different incense sticks.
So, again not knowing which would be best, she grabbed a small bag from next to her bed, placed the crystals in the bottom, then chucked a few different boxes of incense in.
Frankincense, lavender, sage. "One of those must do the job." She thought.

For the last two items on Luna's list, Abi ran down the last flight of stairs and into the kitchen.
She filled a bottle of water, knowing that if she just filled a bowl with water, that she would just spill it on her return to the library. So she filled the bottle with water, grabbed a glass bowl from her baking cupboard and placed both items into the bag.
Finally, a black candle.
Normally, Abi only had white pillar candles that she would place on the fireplace, but luckily, as it was her birthday not too many days ago, she had actually been gifted a beautiful smelling Yankee candle, that just so happened to be black.
Placing the final item into her bag, she hurried back up to the library.

"Got it all," Abi said, passing the bag over to Luna.

Luna started taking the items out of the bag, but one item was still missing. The chalk.

"There's no chalk," Luna informed her after placing the last item onto the floor next to her.
"Oh damn it!" Abi replied.
"Hang on!" Ben exclaimed.

He walked over to the corner of the room where he had left a toolbox when he was helping to fix up the house. Opening up the case, he takes one small piece of chalk out that he had used to mark out placements on the wall for the bookcases.

"Will this do?" He asked, holding up a small thin piece of chalk.

"Perfect!" Luna called out.

"Okay, so we're all set then," She said, as she took the piece of chalk from Ben's hand.

Chapter 24

Luna took the piece of chalk and started drawing out a large star on the wooden panelled floor before encasing it within a circle. By drawing the circle around the pentagram, it brought all of the elements together to work as one combined energy.

"This symbol is one of protection. It enables me to work with the elements with great power and protection against any ill will or negative energies that may try to come through." Luna explained as she finished drawing the pentacle out and standing in the middle.
"Abi, please pass me the other items. I will place one on each point, apart from the top point. The top point symbolises the spirit energy."

Abi passed the items individually to Luna and she placed one on each point. The black candle symbolised fire and of course the colour black to act as protection, a clear quartz crystal to represent the earth from which it came. She poured the water from the bottle into a bowl and placed it at another point to represent the element of water.
Then finally the incense stick was placed on the final point to represent air.

Once all items were in place, she then took a lighter from her pocket and lit the black candle before moving onto the incense.
She chose frankincense, as again it is a protection incense that can also be used to repel bad spirits.

She lit the incense and started moving it in a motion around herself as she sat in the middle of the pentacle.

"Ancestors from the past,
Please join me fast.
Spirit guides all around,
Please keep this protection bound.
Help us connect with James Taylor,
As I wish it, so mote it be."

Luna finished speaking her ritual and called out to James.

"James Taylor, we call out to you. Please come forward. We ask for you to come to us with the highest respect."

The room stayed still and silent.

"Abi, please stand in the pentagram with me. I want to try something. I have a feeling this will work." Luna asked, following her intuition.

Abi stepped into the pentagram and Luna held onto her hands.
"Call out Abi. I think he will come forward for you. You have the blood connection." She assured her.
"Okay." She replied nervously.
"James. I'm your great-granddaughter. Please come through. I want to speak to you about Katrina." Abi closed her eyes and felt an energy build up inside her as she willed for him to come forward.
She suddenly felt prickles all over her body and her eyes shot open.

There before the four of them, was James.
He was dressed in a suit, with what appeared to be blood on his head.

"James?" Abi whispered.
"My dear Abi, you are as beautiful as my dear, sweet Katrina."
He smiled kindly at Abi, but as soon as Katrina's name left his lips, his facial expression changed.
"Katrina." He repeated, but this time his voice said her name with disgust.
"How could she just do that to me? She just ran off and never came back. I did so much for her and tried to get the best help for her."

"She tried to James." Abi assured him.

"She wanted to go home to you and Henry so much. She went through torture at that place. They weren't helping her, they were hurting her. Helen was behind it all. She made out that Katrina was crazy so that she could have you to herself. On the day of Katrina's release, Helen killed her before she could make it home to you and ruined her plans to be reunited. Katrina has been stuck at the Asylum ever since."

"I know Helen was besotted by me. She abducted my son and gave him away. But never would I have thought she was capable of killing Katrina." James replied, confusion in his voice.

"James, do you remember how you died?" Luna asked.

James stayed silent with a puzzled look upon his face.

"I can't remember." He replied.

"What about your head?" Luna indicated to the dried blood amongst his dark hair. He reached up, felt around his head and touched the crusted blood that clumped his black hair together. As he did, he remembered his fall down the stairs and the person who caused his death.

"Helen!" He said in complete outrage. "That evil wench."

"She has killed in life and death and you weren't the last to die at her hands. She has attempted to take our lives too and succeeded with Jack. We can't let it happen anymore."

"How do I know you're telling me the truth about where Katrina's body is? I've been lied to by so many women. How do I know I can trust you? Show me her body. Take me to her." James demanded.

"It's dangerous." Luna said. "She already took Jack away from me and our unborn baby. We can't risk another life."

"I'll show you." Abi volunteered.

"Abi!" Luna called out.

"Just me, no one else. I'm not risking any other lives."

"No, you're not going alone Abi. I'm coming with you. You can't stop me." Ben said adamantly.

"And I'm already dead." Jack said frankly. "What more can she do to me? She's already taken away all that she could from me."

"Thank you, guys. Luna, I need you to stay safe. You have done so much to help us today, but we can't ask you to get any more involved than you already are." Abi said.

"Agreed." Jack continued. "You need to be strong and take care of yourself for our baby."

A tear rolled down Luna's cheek as she held back more sobs.

"I can't talk any of you out of it can I?" She asked, already knowing the answer to her question.

"I'm sorry Luna, I need to end this. Even if it ends with me, at least she won't be able to hurt anyone else."

"Please, keep them safe." She asked Jack. "I love you, I wish I could bring you back."

"I will. And I'll always be here with you hunnie." Jack replied. He moved his hand towards her shoulder, wishing he could feel her skin one last time.

He placed his hand on top of her shoulder and she felt a cold pressure upon her skin.

"I can feel you!" Luna said excitedly. "Well, sort of. I can feel a chill where your hand is. It's sort of sparkly, like a feeling that electricity is close to my skin."

"Well that's how you'll know I'm around then. Every time you feel that, even if you can't see me, you'll know it's me."

"Why won't she see you?" Abi asked curiously.

"Spirits energy won't always be this prominent. Energy can deplete completely which is why you cannot always see spirits. It takes a lot of energy for them to show themselves." Luna replied, her sad eyes gazing at Jack.

"So we need to get a move on. I hate to interrupt this touching moment but didn't you bring me here to get this done?" James interrupted. "As she said, it takes a lot of energy for me to be here." He then pointed over at Jack. "Why don't you and I go to the asylum? As that is where I suppose you came from, you should know a way back there. We can go to the asylum and wait for you two to get there." James finished.

"Oh uh, yeah okay. Sorry." Abi stumbled.

"Please be careful, all of you." Luna pleaded with them. "Here, take this. You'll need it more than I do."

She pulled her necklace over her head and held it out to Abi.
Attached to the chain was a small glass bottle with what looked like oil of some type and some herbs.

"It's a protection bottle. I have made it myself with good intentions of protection for the wearer. It contains Sweet Orange essential oil and rosemary. You can either just wear it as it is, or if you wish, unscrew it and pour a little on your skin to repel bad energies."

"Thank you, Luna. We will be careful. I promise I won't let her take anyone else." Abi said, giving Luna a hug.

Chapter 25

No longer needing all the equipment that they had initially required on their first visit to the asylum, Abi and Ben packed a bag each with some spare clothes just in case, again just some comfy and practical clothes.

"Don't forget the torches." Abi reminded Ben.

The sun was now very low in the sky and Abi's stomach started growling at her.

"I made these." Luna said, walking into the bedroom. "I know it's not much but I thought you both better have something to eat before you leave. I hope you don't mind me raiding your kitchen.
"Oh my god, did you read my mind?" Abi said, reaching out for the sandwich Luna had made for her.

She sat on the bed and took a bite.

"mmm, pate." She said between chewing.
"I felt you were more of a pickle person, Ben, so I made cheese and pickle for you." Luna said, passing Ben the plate.
"Thank you Luna, and yes, spot on." He smiled and took the sandwich.

"My sister will be here soon to give me a lift home. Here is my home number in case you need any advice or if you just need me okay." Luna passed a piece of paper with her phone number to Abi, just as she heard a horn blast twice out the front.

"Well that's her. I'll let myself out. Please come home in one piece." She begged one last time, as she hugged each of them before heading out of the bedroom door.

Abi watched out the window as Luna walked down the garden path and to her sister's car, pulled up on the side of the pathway.
Feeling eyes on her, Luna looked up at the window to see Abi looking down and waved her goodbye before climbing into the car.

"I wish there was something we could do for her." Abi sighed sadly as she waved back at Luna.

"We are. We are going to end this once and for all. We are going to send Jack's killer's soul to the depths of hell, where she belongs and when that's done, we will be here for her. We will help her with the baby and anything else she may need us for. We will help her."

They hold on to each other, the thoughts of either of them not being there, not worth thinking about.
"Right, come on then. Let's do this." Abi said, giving him a final squeeze.

They both grabbed a bag each, filled with their spare clothes and torches and headed down the stairs.

Outside, the low sun rays hit Ben's car windscreen, sending a beam of light straight into their eyes when they opened the front door. After their eyes had readjusted after being almost blinded, they could see the bright oranges flooding the late summer sky.

Ben took her hand and walked down the pathway to the car, opened the passenger side door for her and held her hand as she climbed in.
Ben climbed into the driver's side and pulled away towards the sun and headed out onto the main road.

This time, there was no waiting around. They headed straight to the Asylum. No stopping for breaks, food or drink.

It soon became dark and stars glittered in the now night sky. Streetlamps flickered on, one by one, as they drove down the bypass, giving light to the black roads below.
Abi's head lay against the cold glass window as she stared up at the stars.
Gazing up, she made a wish on as many stars as she could.

Please bring us home safely.
Please help us have strength.
Please guide us.

She repeated it over and over in her head as she focused on each star. This became such a pattern on their journey that Abi drifted off to sleep.

"Abi?" Ben whispered, as he gently shook her knee to wake her.
"Hmm." Abi mumbled as she stirred from her short sleep.
"We're here."

Abi opened her eyes and there before them was the asylum, the driveway lit up by the car headlights.
Mist seemed to circle in patterns through the streaming lights ahead of them.
Ben stepped into the cloudy air. There was an icy chill in the air which was uncommon for that time of year.
The world seemed eerily silent.

Abi shut the car door behind her, making Ben jump as it slammed in the silence.

"Jeez Abi." Ben exclaimed after jumping out of his skin.
"Sorry baby." She apologised.
"Why is it always foggy when we're here?" Ben asked, remembering the last time they were there, trying to get away from the building.

"So we need to try and find James and Jack." Abi began. "Why don't we go to the well where I had that vision and try calling on them there."
"Yeah sure." He replied.

They start heading in the direction of where they believed they remembered the well to be.

Now not having the light from the car, which Ben had purposefully left on, he grabbed the torches from his bag and passed one to Abi so they could see where they were heading through the thick fog.

They switched them on hoping to see better, but all they illuminated was a white sheet of fog ahead of them.

The light did nothing. It was as if they were walking through walls of snow.

Visibility of the path ahead was none existent.

Abi grabbed Ben's hand with her free one, scared of tripping and losing her way.

They walked together hand in hand, trying not to stumble over their own feet, or anything else that may cross their path, however they couldn't avoid the obstacle right ahead.

They didn't know until it was too late.

Ben had fallen straight over a big, bushy shrub in front of him, flipping over onto the ground on the other side and dragged Abi with him.

Groans came from the pair of them as they lay on the grass.

Rubbing their heads from the bumps on the ground, they then looked up to notice the fog seemed to be clearing slightly.

Where they had stumbled, they soon realised was the opening between the trees where the well was located.

How they had not walked into one of the many trees was unknown and they were very lucky to stumble where they did.

They pulled themselves up and brushed off the dry dirt and dead leaves from their clothes.

They could see the faint outline of the well ahead of them and slowly made their way towards it. The twigs cracked beneath their feet as they reached the well.

Abi placed her hands on the cold, damp stone. The moss, wet and fluffy, stuck between the cracks of the old grey bricks.

Her eyes fell to the floor as she noticed something out of the ordinary.

She bent down to investigate the glistening powder at the bottom of the stone circle.

"Salt?" She questioned.

She dabbed her finger on top of the damp crystals and then touched the tip of her tongue to distinguish whether she was right.

"Abi don't do that you don't know what it is, it could be poison for all you know?"

But it was too late. Abi had already put the unknown substance in her mouth.

"It's salt!" She confirmed, brushing the remnants from her hands onto her trousers.

"Well you're lucky then. That could have been anything." Ben sighed.

"But why would there be salt here?" She questioned.

"Isn't salt used for protection?" Ben asked.

"Yes, to keep spirits out... or to keep them in. If Helen got rid of the body in here, I doubt she'd want her soul to be free either. She could be completely trapped down there." Abi cried.

"Well we need to get her out, but how do we even get down there? We have no rope, there's no sign of James or Jack and if there's salt in the grounds around the well, even they can't get down there to see her." Jack explained.

"Wait." Abi exclaimed, trying to bring a memory back to her mind.

"When we were last here, at the asylum I mean, not the well. The first time we gained access inside, we had to go through those tunnels. Don't you remember? There was a skeleton at the end of one of them. What if that was Katrina? What if that was the bottom of the well and there is an underground tunnel that links to it?!"

"It was very wet down there. It could be that the tunnels were what fed water to the well." He theorised, remembering the trickles of water running down the shiny stone walls.

"We need to get back down there Ben."

"What about Jack and James?" He asked.

"What if we try summoning them?" She suggested.

"I have a little knowledge of how to do it after speaking with Luna."

"I mean, yeah, we could give it a try I suppose." Ben shrugged.

She took the quartz crystals that Luna had given her from her bag and placed them in a circle around the pair of them.

They held each other's hands and closed their eyes.

"I call upon the goddesses and gods.
I call upon the elements.
I call upon north, south, east and west.
Bring forward those we ask of.
Bring Forward James.
Bring forward Jack.
As I say it, so mote it be."

After speaking these words they opened their eyes.

Nothing. No one.

"Hmm, well that didn't work. Should we try again?" Ben asked.
"Yes. Maybe now that you know what to say, we could try doing it together?"
"Yeah, okay." He replied.
"Okay, so close your eyes and imagine a white light surrounding the both of us in a bubble and speak along with me." She explained.
In unison, they both repeated the words.

"I call upon the goddesses and gods.
I call upon the elements.
I call upon north, south, east and west.
Bring forward those we ask of.
Bring forward James.
Bring forward Jack.
As I say it, so mote it be."

They held their eyes shut for longer this time, waiting for something to happen. The wind around them picked up and swirled, throwing sticks and leaves all around them, as though they were in the eye of a storm.

The area became silent and they opened their eyes.

The debris floated around in the air, but as if in slow motion. Abi and Ben looked at each other in confusion.

"You called?" Jack said humorously.

Everything dropped back down to the earth and Abi and Ben turned around to find Jack and James standing behind them.

"Seriously?" Abi cried out after jumping out of her skin. "You scared me half to death."
"Luckily we didn't scare you to ACTUAL death then hey? Otherwise you'd be joining our little dead club here wouldn't you." Jack chuckled.
"Not funny Jack." Ben shot him a look as if to say, pack it in Jack.
"Alright, alright. I'm sorry." Jack apologised.
"So what's the plan? I do take it you have one." James asked.
"Jack, do you remember the tunnels under the asylum?" Abi asked.
"Yes of course I remember that dank place, what of it?"

"We believe it connects to the well." She started.

"Why can't we just go straight down the well?" James questioned.

"Well, for one we don't have a way down there, no ladder, no rope, nothing. And two, it has salt protection so you and Jack can't get in from above. So the only way in would be from below and I remember seeing a skeleton down there and I'm hoping it's Katrina." Abi explained.

"So we need to go back inside?" Jack asked nervously.

"I'm afraid so." Abi confirmed.

They all looked up at the building as the fog started to disperse, revealing the moonlit Asylum through the intertwining trees.

They started to make their way towards the steps of the building, careful not to have another fall on the way and add more bumps and bruises to their already sore bodies.

They climbed the few rickety steps to the main entrance doors. The last time they were at these doors, was when Ben had got Abi outside for some fresh air after all of the commotion with Jack.

Ben placed his hand on the cold brass handle of the door and pushed it open. It opened with a creek and seemed to scratch along the floor as it revealed the reception hall and desk.

There was broken furniture all around. An old bench seat towards the entrance, that once would have been seating for those visiting the hospital and its patients, laid in two pieces on the dusty ground. It had red upholstered buttoned material that would have once looked royal and vibrant, but now ripped to shreds and filled with years and years of built-up dust and dirt.

There were bits of wood everywhere that may have once been furniture, but due to the state of the pieces, you would never be able to tell. There were also cracks throughout the tiled flooring, meaning they had to watch their step in this area. It was a death trap just waiting for its next victims.

Ben led the others through into the reception area, stepping over the pieces of debris and pointing out broken, sharp shards of glass to Abi.

"Watch yourself. This place is dangerous." He warned, taking her hand and guiding her over the glassy mess.

They all stood in the middle of the room, dust particles floating around them in the air.

"Do you remember which way it was to the trap door?" Abi asked Ben, her memory starting to fail her.
Ben racked his brains. Their first visit was so intense and dramatic that it was hard to remember what happened when and where.
"Maybe this way?" He said, not entirely confident in his decision.

They headed towards the reception desk and walked behind it. There were papers everywhere. Most so dirty that you couldn't even make out the writing.

On the desk amongst the dirt and papers was an old telephone.
Nowadays, a corded telephone was very rarely seen.

Abi was mesmerised by it. It was black with a round brass dial that had holes, through the holes you could just about make out faded numbers.
She put her hand out to touch it, but before even getting her hand on the receiver, it rang.

Abi jumped back, the phone's loud ring scared the hell out of her.
She edged back toward it and picked up the receiver from its dusty base and brought it to her ear slowly, scared of what she would hear.

"H... Hello?" She stammered anxiously.

There was a shallow crackling noise coming through like white noise from a T.V.

"Hello, is there anyone there?" She asked again, waiting for a voice to come through the static sounds.
"You can't save her!" A gruff voice came through.

Abi threw the phone as quick as she could as soon as she heard the words hitting her ears.

"Helen!" She screamed at the rest of the group.
"It was Helen. She said we can't save her, she's going to try and stop us from helping Katrina."
"Not on my watch darling." James said sternly, pulling his waistcoat down and rolling his shirt sleeves up as though he was preparing for a fight.

"She will no longer mess with my family."

James was quite angry and ready to take his revenge.

"Count me in!" Jack agreed, "I've had enough of this wench getting her way and messing with people's lives. Enough is enough." And mirrored James by rolling his sleeves up too.
"We will help her Abi." Ben comforted her.

"Come on, let's try through here." Ben directed, as he nodded in the direction of a doorway behind the reception desk.
He took her hand and led her through the doorway into the next room.
The door was laying on the floor in front of the,, giving them slight deja vu as they stepped over it.

They stepped into the musty smelling room that seemed to be slightly recognisable.
They took a look around and noticed the name plaque on the desk and the files around the room.

Dr Arthur Watson.

"We're here!" Abi said in relief. "The trap door is in here somewhere, remember? This was the first room we entered when we arrived the last time we came here."

They started looking around the floor, kicking pieces of paper that hid the wooden floorboards beneath them.
Dust filled the room from where they had disturbed it on the floor. It had been sat there, silently alone since they had last been in there, causing Ben to sneeze.

As Ben closed his eyes to sneeze, he tripped over a stack of books landing face-first into the wooden planks below him.
As he stuck his hands out to stop him from hitting the floor entirely, his hands landed on something metal.

"A handle!" Ben exclaimed, after his sneezing fit had finished.
"Guys, it's over here! I've found it!"

Everyone stopped searching and fled to where Ben had fallen.
Pushing all of the papers out of the way, there before them was the trap door to the tunnels below.

Jack pulled the old iron handle up, pushing the door away from him, revealing the dark depths of the tunnels.
Cold air rushed up from the darkness and the wind moaned as it flowed through to the room.

"In you go then." Jack said. "What are we waiting for?"
"I'm going, give me a chance." Ben replied.

He pushed the door so that it slammed backwards with a loud thud.
He turned around and slowly started to lower himself down onto the ladder and as he touched it, he remembered the last time he was in the tunnels.

"Ugh, I forgot how wet it was down here." He said, disgusted with the liquid now on his hands.

He carried on further down the ladder, each step he took echoed through the tunnels.
Abi started to make her way down after him, while James and Jack met them at the bottom of the tunnel, not having to make their way down the ladder themselves.

"We need to go this way and then when we get to the end, start climbing the ladder up. There should be another tunnel coming off to the right as you climb. That tunnel will lead us to the inner well where I saw the body." She instructed, as she remembered the first time she had come across the skeleton.
It was on a ledge with one arm dangling into the water of the well.

They reached the turning after starting to climb the last ladder and followed it down to the well, bending over slightly as it started to narrow.
Their hands against the wet, sparkling walls as they continued. The light of their only torch reflected off of the droplets running down the walls.

The light flickered.
Ben hit the side of the torch and it came back to life, so he continued leading the way forward.
A few steps more and the torchlight went completely out. With no light, their other senses became heightened and they noticed the sound of water.
Not the water dripping down the walls, but what sounded like rainwater falling ahead of them.

"I think we're close." Abi said, still holding onto the walls, even more now that there was no light to guide them.

A loud bang roared through the tunnels making them all jump.

"Thunder!" Abi cried out.

The rain suddenly became harder, sounding like a waterfall and the water now collecting around their feet.

"Ben quick! Before we drown!" She shouted to him.

They ran, or at least tried to, blindly forwards as the water rose quickly up their legs, making it harder for them to make their way to the well.

The water now gushing in, was attempting to push them back, but they didn't give up, they continued to push through and finally saw the water rushing down in front of them like a waterfall.

"The well! We've made it!" Ben shouted over the noise of the water crashing down.
"But we will never make it back to the end of the tunnel and up to the surface." Abi cried.
"We won't have to Abi." Ben replied. "We grab Katrina's skeleton and float to the top of the well."
"James, Jack, we will meet you back at the top" He continued.
"So we weren't even needed down here in the first place?" James said, a little frustrated.
"No, and it doesn't matter! We are not arguing about it now! Go!" Ben shouted back at him.

Ben jumped into the water ahead, plunging into the depths of the well, his head going under the murky water and bobbing back up again with a gasp.
He floated in the water looking for the ledge that Abi had mentioned.

"There's no ledge Abi! Are you sure it was this tunnel?" He shouted over to her.
"Yes, 100 percent. It's probably underwater Ben!" She shouted back, the water now approaching her hips.
"Of course it is." Ben sighed.

Knowing exactly what had to be done, he took a deep breath and dove under the water.

There she was. Ben had found Katrina's skeleton. It was stuck on the ledge that Katrina had said about. Her arm seemingly wanted to float to the top of the water, but the rest of her was trapped by bottles and other bits of rubbish that people had dumped down the well.

He swam over to her and removed the rubbish from her and her body was released. He grabbed her and kicked his feet as fast as he could, he swam back to the surface of the water with Katrina in his arms.

He reached the surface and took the biggest breath.

"I've got her!" Ben called out.

He started to pass the bones over to Abi while he caught his breath, but mid pass, his head quickly shot back underwater.

"Ben!" Abi called out.

His body was rushing down into the depths of the water.

Looking down, he could see a body dragging him down and the sound of sinister laughter around him in the water, as it was rushing up past his body.

It was Helen.

She was dragging him down in an attempt to stop him from getting Katrina to the surface.

Ben thrashed his feet, kicking as hard and as fast as he possibly could, to try and free himself, but it wasn't enough.

She had him in her grips with no way out.

Bubbles now flowing quickly out of Ben's mouth, making their way up past his face, like bubbles in a water cooler.

As the last breath left his body with one large bubble, Ben drifted to the bottom of the well, unconscious.

Abi saw a collection of bubbles popping on the surface. She dropped Katrina's body without a thought and dove in after Ben.

The water was so murky, that Ben was barely visible at the bottom of the watery pit.

185

Finally reaching him, Abi grabbed hold of Ben in one arm, bent down low and pushed off the ground as hard as she could, propelling herself and Ben to the surface of the water.

The water was still rising but a rope ladder had appeared right at her side, as she floated.

She clutched hold of the ladder and climbed up, Ben's weight now taking a toll on her as she carried his water-soaked body to the opening of the well.

Finally reaching the top, she placed Ben's body over the edge and he began coughing. Water escaped his body, freeing his lungs so that they could now fill with air and he could breathe again.

"Ben, I'll be right back okay. You'll be fine. I need to get Katrina!"

Ben continued to cough and weakly rose his hand to grab her, but it was too late.

"Wait." He spluttered.

But she didn't hear him. She climbed back down the ladder and as she neared the water, she dove back in. This time to rescue Katrina.

Katrina's body was slowly swaying down to the bottom of the well and Abi hadn't thought about how much the water had risen.
This time, she had a long way to go.

Abi's lungs began to feel tight and she wanted more than anything to gasp for some air, but down here, there wasn't any.
Just water and more filthy water.

She finally reached Katrina's body, taking it in her arms and turning back to aim for the water's surface one last time. However, there was nothing for her to propel from. The base of the well was further down and she wouldn't make it. She flicked her feet below her, thrashing them backwards and forwards in an attempt to gain some speed as she swam upwards.

The pressure was building in her head and before she even knew it, her mouth was wide open, choking down water. Her body had involuntarily opened up as she suffocated, in hopes of air, but instead, her poor lungs were filling with rushing, dirty water.

Her body was now full of water, her brain starved of oxygen, she floated unconsciously in the water, her eyes wide open and Katrina's bones still locked in her arms, as if they were in a watery embrace.

Light shone around the two of them and a faint voice came through.

"I won't leave you Abi. You will be safe. You helped me, you saved me. It's my turn to save you."
It was Katrina. Her hair flowed around her like an angelic mermaid, moving slowly closer to Abi.
"I will save you."

Her spirit fell into Abi's body and after a few seconds of silence, Abi's body seemed to wake up and as if shocked with a bolt of lightning, energy soared through her and she swam as fast as she could to the surface of the well.

As she broke free, water exploded from her lips.

Abi choked as the water flowed from her lungs, out of her mouth so that she was once again breathing clearly.
For a few seconds, she lay at the top of the still watery surface.

The rain had calmed and gently pattered onto her face, leaving her feeling a lot calmer after the madness that had just occurred.

"Abi?" Ben called out. His voice now clearer after his choking episode.
"Abi are you okay?" He called down to where Abi was floating in the water.

He started climbing down the ladder, carefully making his way down to her. The water had risen so much, that he didn't have to climb down far at all. He reached out to her and slowly pulled her towards him.

Abi's energy had completely drained and she was left feeling tired and heavy. Her body aching, Ben helped her onto the ladder and out of the well.
She handed the skeleton over to Ben and laid down on the muddy grass, not bothered about her clothes getting dirty at all. She needed the rest.

"Katrina saved me." She whispered, as her eyes fluttered shut.

"She saved me"

Chapter 26

Ben had already been back to his car to grab supplies for when she got out of the well. He pulled a top from his bag and dried off Abi's face.

"You did it," Ben said in a hushed, calming voice.
"You got Katrina out of that watery grave."
"So it's true." James sighed, as a tear ran down his face.
He was staring off into the distance, although they didn't realise why at first.

A womanly shadow was coming closer to them through the low sitting fog. The vapour swirled around her as she came closer.

"Oh my love." James cried out.

He ran over to the beautiful woman before them and whisked her off her feet, spinning her around as if they were dancing in the clouds.
He brought her in close.

"Oh Katrina, I am so sorry. I should never have sent you to this god awful place. I should have believed you." His tone then changed. He became angry.
"That wretched woman!" He growled.

"Oh why thank you so much, James." A sarcastic voice came from behind the trees.

"Aww look at the reunited couple, happy together at last." She hissed.

"You have no place here Helen!" James spat.

"Take yourself back to the horrid PIT you came from"

"Do you really think I'd let either of you move on! Ha!" Helen laughed bitterly.

James threw himself at Helen and their bodies twisted together in a blurred flash, as they fought each other in fury.

To onlookers, all they could see was a twist of lights, both white and black swishes and merging with aggression.

"Stop! James stop! This is what she wants! She feeds off of emotion and anger! Stop!" Katrina's voice pierced through the anger charged air around them.

The twisting colours fell apart where James had stopped, but Helen hadn't given up.

Stronger than before, she had James by his throat, pinned to the ground.

"What are you going to do Helen? Kill me? You've already done that!" James laid there.

He was fed up now. What more could she seriously do? She had tortured his wife, given away their son, killed Katrina and himself and put his descendants in danger.

Helen had gone quiet.

Taking advantage of her silence, James kicked her from his transparent body and she fell against the side of the well.

Her hand fell onto the salt sodden ground and her hand began to burn and sizzle.

"Shit!" She exclaimed. She rushed her hand from the salty ground and rolled further away.

"Abi! The crystals Luna gave you.. they can trap her can't they?!" Jack whispered to her excitedly.

"Yes!" She crawled over to her bag that Ben had earlier gotten from the car.

She ripped the zip open, grabbed the clear quartz chunks from the depths of the bag and ran over to where Helen lay on the ground.

She placed the 3 crystals around Helen in a triangle and 3 lights shot up encasing Helen in a light-filled pyramid.

Helen touched the light that had entrapped her and she received a surge of

189

electricity through her fingers, making her fall back in quite literal shock.

"What have you done!" She shrieked.
"The truth's out now Helen. You cannot hurt my family OR my friends anymore."

Abi's voice was now full of power and confidence. She pulled one more item from her bag. One that Ben didn't even know she had packed and another gift from Luna.

It was a brown, leather-bound book, which Abi turned to a bookmarked page. The pages were thick and filled with history, recipes and spells.

Abi stood stern and read from the page before her.

"From this day and forevermore,
You are banished behind the un-opening door.
Thrown to the depths of the abyss,
No longer able to destroy others bliss.
For as long as your immortal soul wanders I banish thee,
From now and forever so mote it be!"

The ground began to rumble under their feet, making Abi and Ben grab a hold of one another to steady themselves.

Ahead of them, a loud crash echoed through the trees, as all the windows from the asylum smashed and glass flew in all directions. The asylum ahead began to fall to the ground. The turrets crumbled with large bricks, sending more rumbles through the earth.

With one loud bang, the whole of the asylum was now in ruins, a large crack formed in the ground and it started to run from the building, towards them all in the wooded area of the grounds.
The crack grew so fast, that there was no time to run and before they knew it, it had struck the well wall behind Helen.
The force was so strong that it caused Ben and Abi to fall to the ground.

"No, no, no! You can't take me! I won't go!" Helen screamed, as the ground opened up below her.

She held on so tight to the stones of the well, in hopes of not being sucked into the fires tickling at her feet. But the pull was too strong and her fingertips were failing her.

She struggled to remain attached to the well and clung on with all her strength. She started pulling herself up with her arms, fleeing the hell fire's, but the universe had other ideas.

The storm had started to return with rumbles of thunder overhead.
One large bolt of lightning struck the brick of the well that Helen was clinging on to.

"Noooooooo!" Helen cried, as she fell violently into the mouth of hell.

A blaze of light shot up out of the opening in the ground, causing everyone to hide their eyes.

There was silence all around them.

Abi was first to lift her head from her arms, hiding from the blinding light that had shot up into the sky.
Looking around, the area surrounding them looked no different to when they had first arrived.

The hole in the ground that had swallowed Helen, was no longer there. As if it had all been imagined. Even the crack in the ground had disappeared. It would all have seemed to have been a dream, if it hadn't have been for the missing brick from the top of the well wall.

The sun had just started to come up over the top of the old asylum. The building, now no longer a building. The asylum was now a pile of rubble.
All the souls once trapped here were now free to move on, including James, Katrina and their dear friend Jack.

A ray of beautiful orange sunrise, shone over the asylum directly at the 5 of them.

Katrina and James fully embraced each other at last.
Katrinas face turned toward Ben and Abi.

"Abi." She started. "I am so sorry for putting you through this nightmare. I had tried for years to get people in our family to notice me. No one ever saw the signs, until one day someone moved into our old home." Katrina looked up at James with a smile.

"Abi, you are the only one who could have helped me, to help us. You know my story now and the truth is out. We can now move on together at last." She smiled warmly.

"Mother? Father?" A young man's voice called forward softly.

He walked towards them and slowly his image changed from what was once a suited gentleman, into a small child wearing brown shorts and a white shirt.

"Henry?" Katrina questioned. Her heart was beating fast and a tear fell down her cheek.

The little boy went running up to them with his arms held open wide.

"Oh, my dear boy!" James cried, as he knelt low.

Henry ran into his arms and James lifted him into the air and held him tighter than he had ever held him before.
Katrina in sobs of relief held onto them both, feeling so thankful to have both of her boys back, finally.

"Thank you Abi, and of course Ben. This could never have happened without you." James said, tears wet on his face.
"You will never know how much this means to us. You will forever have our protection sweet Abi." James and Katrina walked towards them, Henry in his mother's arms.
"Always." Katrina whispered lovingly.

But before Abi could even reply, they faded into the sunset, their souls disappearing before their eyes.
They both looked quickly towards Jack to make sure he hadn't disappeared on them as well. Thankfully he was still there.

"I guess it's my turn to say goodbye." Jack said softly.
"I don't know what's beyond that light." he started, looking directly into the suns warming rays.
"But, if there is any chance I can come back for visits, even if you can't see me, be sure I will be back and I'll send loads of signs that I'm there. I promise." He said.
"I'm sure you will." Abi giggled softly, imagining him causing chaos.

"Just nothing too jumpy hey mate." Ben smiled at jack.

"Haha I'll try not to make you wet yourself mate, don't worry." Jack laughed.

"Look after Luna will you, both of you. And the baby. My son."

"You think you'll have a boy?" Abi asked, surprised.

"Yeah definitely! A little football player." He smiled to himself.

"Tell him stories of his dad won't you?. All the things we got up to as kids?" Jack motioned to Ben.

"Of course I will. Every single adventure and I won't leave out any details of how stupid his dad could be." He smiled.

"Thanks Ben. Thank you both."

Jack took a few steps back, still smiling, he gave them a wave before walking towards the sun and disappearing into the rays before them.

Epilogue

"Happy birthday little Jack!" Abi greeted, excitedly.

They had just arrived at Luna's for her son's 1st birthday. The sun was shining bright and beautiful. It was mid-May and the weather couldn't be better for them. There was a bouncy castle on the lawn for the older children and mocktails for the parents next to the barbecue area.

"Thank you so much for making his cake Abi!" Luna said appreciatively. "It looks delicious."

Abi had made him a jungle-themed cake with little figurines of a tiger, an elephant and a monkey, all made from icing, sitting on top of a white iced cake and a number one candle stuck in beside them.

"You're welcome. Only the best for our little Jack hey!" She beamed, as she placed the cake on the table in the shade.

She turned around and saw silent tears falling from Luna's eyes.

"Hey what's wrong Luna?" Abi asked gently, taking hold of her arm and walking into the kitchen.
"I just wish Jack was here." She replied, picking up a frame showing the two of them in each other's arms at a family member's wedding.
"Oh hunnie." Abi said softly.

She pulled Luna into a warm hug. Luna's tears fell onto Abi's shoulders.

"He will be here, Luna. One of the last things he said to us was that he would visit. It's his son's 1st birthday, he wouldn't miss it for the world, dead or alive. You know that." She said softly, trying to comfort her.

"I know. It's just been so hard without him. I tell Jack of his dad all the time, not that he would understand." Luna replied.

THUD.

A loud bang thumped above their heads and the pair of them almost jumped out of their skins.

Both of their heads shot straight up, to a point on the ceiling from where they had heard the noise.

"You don't think...?" Abi started.

"Let's go check." Luna suggested, her grip on Abi tightening.

"Ben, we'll be back down in a bit!" Abi called out into the garden.

Ben nodded back to show all was good and he had things under control with the kids, who were currently climbing all over him.

Abi and Luna headed up the stairs, Abi holding her long white skirt off the floor, so she didn't trip on her way up the cream carpet stairs.

They got to the landing and turned left into the main bedroom.

Opening the door, the room was full of light.

The walls were white with hints of purple throughout the decor. Her bedding was violet, with white scatter cushions and an astrology tapestry hanging on the wall above the bed.

On her dressing table, was a vase overflowing with fragrant lavender, which filled the room with its calming smell.

The drawer of the dresser was on the floor. A box from the drawer had fallen open and its contents were scattered all over.

"Jack?" Luna questioned softly.

A breeze came in through the window and revealed some papers that had escaped the box.

Luna picked up the pages.

The will and testament of Jack Winters.

"Abi.. I.. I.. I cant." Luna said, handing the papers over to Abi.
"Oh, Luna." She said as she read the first line. "Maybe we should get the party out of the way and read this with Ben."
"Yeah." She sighed, as she tried to pull herself together.

Abi held onto the papers until the party was over.

It got to 4 pm and Abi poured the three of them a glass of wine, whilst Luna put baby Jack to bed.

"So while you were outside with the kids earlier, we heard a noise upstairs so went to check it out. We found this on the floor. It had fallen out of a box in one of the drawers." She pulled out the will from her handbag on the kitchen side and passed it to Ben.
"I knew he would have done a will. Even though he could be a complete idiot at times, he was smart. He always had a backup plan for anything that went wrong," Ben said, as he read the will.
"Woah! Abi have you read this yet?" He asked in amazement.
"No. Why what's up?" Abi replied, concerned by the look of shock on his face.

Luna made her way down the stairs leading into the living room.
Abi passed her a glass of wine and they all sat down on the sofa to go over what they had found.

"Okay." Luna said, taking a deep breath. "Let's get this over with."
"So I've looked through the document and I'm just going to just get this done, rather than going through all the law mumbo jumbo stuff. Luna..." Ben started.

Abi took luna's hand tightly.

"Ben has left this letter for you." He said pulling a letter out from the paperwork."Would you like me to read it?" He asked softly.
Luna nodded.

"My dear Luna,

I'm sorry if you're reading this letter, as it would mean that I am no longer here.
I want you to know that you were, are and forever will be my world.
I wrote this early in life, you know what I'm like with being prepared and when I

live in this world of paranormal mess, we never know what's going to happen.
So, of course, I have something set aside for you.
Go into the bedroom, pick up the rug on my side of the bed. There is a loose
floorboard where I've hidden something for you.
Find it before reading on"

Ben stopped reading the letter.

"Seriously?" Luna said. "He would get me looking for stuff." She huffed, as she
placed her glass down on the coffee table in front of them.
"Come on then, on the treasure hunt we go."

They all made their way back up to the bedroom and Luna flipped the light switch,
filling the room with a warming, cosy light.

Luna headed over to Jack's side of the bed and lifted the rug. There before her,
were scratches all over the woodwork and the plank he was talking about was
quite visible to anyone looking for a hiding place. It was the only one without
scratches all over it, even though all the planks surrounding it were damaged.

Bending down to look at the floorboard, she noticed a screwdriver hidden under
the bed that was used to lift the floorboard.
She grabbed it by the rubber handle and stuck the flat end into the small gap
between the wooden boards and levered it up.
She picked the board up and placed it to one side as she gasped.

"Oh my god." She whispered.
She placed her hand into the hole in the floor and brought up a pile of cash.

"There's more down there!" She was in complete shock.

Jack had left her piles upon piles of cash under the floorboards.

"Ben, what did the rest of the letter say?" Luna asked. They were all in shock.

"Oh uh...." He stumbled as he looked back down at the letter.
"Don't freak out, I didn't rob a bank. I saved this from all the investigation work I
did for others, as well as an inheritance from my grandfather. I've been saving up
for our future, our wedding and our family. I wanted you to have the best of
everything darling, whether that's with or without me.
197

There should be enough to pay off the mortgage and some extra.

Please be happy hunnie. Use the money to have a comfortable life. Get everything you ever wanted and know even though I'm gone, I'll always be with you in spirit to enjoy it.

With everything that I have come across in the paranormal, I believe I will be able to come back and send you signs that I'm about when you need me, so keep an eye out for me beautiful.

Know that I will always love you.

Yours always,

Jack.

P.S. Tell Ben to go into my bottom drawer, I have left him something"

Luna stayed, sat on the floor, teardrops falling onto the cash notes in her hands.

"Oh Jack, you always thought of everything. I just wish you were here." She spoke with her head tilted back, looking up towards the ceiling and smiling.
"I love you."

Ben frowned.

He walked towards Jack's old chest of drawers. They hadn't been touched all the time that Jack had been gone.

He crouched down and pulled the bottom drawer open and rummaged through looking for a letter.

He moved a pair of jeans to one side and found a letter with a box.

He opened the letter and read it to himself while Abi comforted Luna.

Hi Ben,

So apparently I'm not invincible after all, hey mate.

Please look after my Luna, she will need friends when I am gone and I could think of no one better to keep an eye out for her than you, my best friend.

I know I'm getting soppy, don't judge me.

Anyway... I want you to have this and go get your girl.

Stop delaying it mate. Life's too short.

Have the best life and know I'll always be looking out for you all.

All my best mate.

Jack.

Ben folded the letter up and placed it in his pocket.

"What did it say, Ben?" Abi asked, still holding onto Luna.

Ben took the box out of the drawer, his back facing them. He opened the small navy coloured box to find the most beautiful tear-drop shaped diamond, set on a white gold band.

"It's perfect mate. Thanks." He whispered.

"Huh?" Luna asked, not hearing a word he had said.

He turned around to face them both.

"Luna, can I talk to you in private for a moment?" He asked.
"Erm, yeah, sure." She was puzzled.
"Oh okay, I'll head back downstairs and grab another glass of wine. Would you both like a top-up?" Abi asked.
"Yes please." They replied in unison.

Abi took the glasses and headed out the door.

"I'll meet you both back down here when you're ready." Abi said with a small smile.

Abi made her way down the stairs and into the kitchen to top up their glasses and took them into the front room.
It was getting quite chilly down there now, so Abi popped a log on the fire and wrapped a cardigan around her shoulders.
It was unusual for it to feel this cold at this time of year, it should be warm enough to not have the heating on at all, let alone the fire.

All the hairs on Abi's arms stood on end and she felt as though someone was watching her.
She spun on the spot, in front of the fireplace to see who was behind her and nearly threw her glass, until she realised who it was.

"Jack?!" She exclaimed. "Bloody hell," she said, grasping at her top and placing the glass down on the table. "Jack, you scared the hell out of me!"
"I'm sorry Abi, I didn't know how to approach you without scaring you." He laughed. "I am a ghost after all." He smiled.

"Oh Jack, Luna is going to be over the moon that you're here. We found your will!"

"I know, I've been watching. That's why I'm here." Jack had the biggest grin on his face.

"What you've done for Luna and baby Jack is amazing Jack. You thought ahead. I haven't even done that. I don't even have life insurance. I really should sort that out. But Jack, it is so good to see you." Abi reached out her arms.

Again she had completely forgotten that she couldn't hug ghosts, so instead of hugging him, she fell straight through him and landed on the sofa.

"I'm not physical Abi." He sat on the sofa to join her and they both sat there laughing.

"Did I just hear laughing?" Luna asked Ben, after their private chat.
"Uh.. yeah.. well, at least I think so." Ben replied.

They both made their way down the stairs to join Abi.

Halfway down, Luna saw Jack sitting on the sofa, and just like Abi, she ran down the stairs to embrace him, but instead face planted the back of the sofa.

"Oh, uh, hey hunnie," He said with a giggle, as she sat inside his apparition.
"I forgot." She said, as she pulled herself up to sit next to him.
"I know, it's okay." He placed his hand just above her knee and closed his eyes.

She could feel a soft, cold air above her knee. It was comforting, not as much as a hug, but as close as it could be to feel his touch.

"Did baby Jack enjoy his birthday?" Jack asked with a small smile.
"He did. He was out like a light when I put him to bed. He looks so much like you." Luna replied.
"Of course he does! Has to get his good looks from his dad, doesn't he?" He laughed.
"So..." He said, looking at Ben. "Get my letter pal?"
Ben smiled."Yes, Jack, I did."

The lights went out and flames flickered onto candlesticks out of nowhere.

"I've been practising." Jack whispered.

The room was filled with light from every candle in the room, and Luna being a witch, meant she had A LOT of candles.

"Abi?" Ben said. He slowly went down onto one knee and the girls gasped.

Luna's hand jumped from her lap, through Jack and onto Abi's knee and vigorously shook it in excitement.

"Oh my god." Abi whispered, a tear rolling down her cheek.
"No... just Ben." Jack sneaked in cheekily. "Sorry, carry on."

Luna now realising that her arm was right through Jack, slowly placed her hand back on her lap and mouthed the word sorry to him.

"Thanks Jack." He laughed.
"Abi. I have loved you since the first moment I ever laid eyes on you. I always knew i'd have to wait for you, but I would wait a million years if it meant I got to marry you one day. So Abi... would you be my wife?" He asked, his heart thumping hard and his palms starting to sweat.
"Of course I will." She pulled him up off his knees and kissed him hard on the lips.

Ben gently pushed the sparkling ring onto her finger and hugged her, as a feeling of relief and love overflowed inside him.

Jack and Luna both cheered loudly and woke baby Jack up.
Luna ran upstairs and got baby Jack.

"We have some exciting news baby boy!" She whispered excitedly.

She took him downstairs to where her best friends and his dad were

"Look who it is, baby! Auntie Abi, Uncle Ben and Daddy! And guess what? Auntie Abi and Uncle Ben are getting married!" She said, bouncing him on her hip.

Although everyone knew baby Jack wouldn't have a clue what was going on, you would never know. He was happy and giggling and clapping his hands together in excitement.

"I have one more surprise." Ben said to them all.

"Abi, Ben. I'm leaving you my business. I know it's not for everyone, but I want you both to take over. It's what brought us all together and I know my clients will adore you both."

"Seriously Jack?" Ben asked and then looked to Abi."What do you reckon hun? Up for some more paranormal investigations?"

Abi pretended to take a second to think about it and blurted out, " Of course! I know it was hard and we went through a lot, but we helped both Katrina and James and of course, little Henry to become a family again and we got the truth out. We learnt so much as well."

"Well, that's it then! You've got a deal. Just promise me one thing, Jack?" Ben asked.

"Don't come into the investigation and play tricks." He smiled. "We know what you're like. We'll be out trying to find evidence and then you pop in and mix up everything."

"I won't, I won't. I promise." Jack replied.

A few weeks later a news article is released regarding the once Jack Winters.

After Jack Winters tragically passed away last year during an investigation of Blue waters Hospital, he passed his successful Ghost Investigation business over to his good friends Ben and Abi.

Jack was a successful ghost hunter with his own youtube channel and clients worldwide.

Thanks to Abi and Ben's hard work, the show goes on and by show, I mean their new T.V programme which can be found on the Horror channel Friday nights at 10 pm. They have already investigated places such as Dover Castle and the Edinburgh Vaults. Where will their journey take them next and will we ever come face to face with the ghost of Jack?

Only time will tell!

The Woman In The Mirror

Printed in Great Britain
by Amazon